Clark Sm

Descriptive Catalogue of Ornamental Trees

Anatiposi

Clark Smith, Powell Smith

Descriptive Catalogue of Ornamental Trees

Reprint of the original, first published in 1871.

1st Edition 2023 | ISBN: 978-3-38212-636-0

Anatiposi Verlag is an imprint of Outlook Verlagsgesellschaft mbH.

Verlag (Publisher): Outlook Verlag GmbH, Zeilweg 44, 60439 Frankfurt, Deutschland
Vertretungsberechtigt (Authorized to represent): E. Roepke, Zeilweg 44, 60439 Frankfurt, Deutschland
Druck (Print): Books on Demand GmbH, In de Tarpen 42, 22848 Norderstedt, Deutschland

No. 2.

Descriptive Catalogue.

ORNAMENTAL

DEPARTMENT.

Syracuse Nurseries,

SMITH, CLARK & POWELL, Proprietors.

[No. 2.]

DESCRIPTIVE CATALOGUE

OF

ORNAMENTAL TREES,

SHRUBS, VINES, ROSES, ETC.,

GREEN HOUSE AND HOT HOUSE PLANTS,

CULTIVATED AND FOR SALE AT THE

SYRACUSE NURSERIES,

Established 1830,

SYRACUSE, N. Y.

Smith, Clark & Powell,

PROPRIETORS.

SYRACUSE:
PRINTED AT THE DAILY JOURNAL OFFICE,
1871.

PREFATORY.

In the Ornamental Department we have a stock of Trees and Plants unsurpassed in quality. In all particulars in this line, we aim to keep fully up with the requirements of the times, which are constantly and rapidly increasing.

The Evergreen and Weeping Trees (Deciduous,) are unrivalled for purposes of Ornamentation for public and private grounds, and of these we shall keep a full supply of the very choicest kinds.

The Floral department in all its branches is fully stocked, and we are prepared to offer a fine list of the best of Green House and Bedding-out Plants, &c., &c.

Visitors are freely invited at all times to make personal examination of our stock.

The usual periods for transplanting with us, are from about the middle of October to the first of December, in the Autumn, and from the last of March to the beginning of May, in the Spring. Trees for the South and West should be forwarded in the Autumn.

Correspondents will please be particular to write out their orders *very distinctly and methodically ; also to specify the route by which they wish their goods sent.* Attention to this hint may save them and us much inconvenience.

All orders from strangers should enclose the cash, or contain a satisfactory reference.

Our office is situated corner of West Genesee and Geddes streets, and easily accessible from the R. R. Station.

CATALOGUES.

Our Catalogues will be sent to all who apply and enclose as follows:—Nos. 1 and 2, each ten cents; No, 3, three cents.

No. 1—A Descriptive Catalogue of Fruits.

No. 2—A Descriptive Catalogue of Ornamental Trees, Shrubs, Roses, &c.

No. 3—A Wholesale Catalogue, or Trade List.

SMITH, CLARK & POWELL.

SYRACUSE, N. Y., 1871.

ORNAMENTAL DEPARTMENT.

Deciduous Trees.

The Prices affixed are for good sized, merchantable Trees, at the Nursery. Extra sized Trees charged for in proportion.

ABELE, SNOWY MAPLE LEAVED.—Rapid grower, foliage large and glossy above, downy white beneath. 50 cents to $1.

ALMOND, LARGE DOUBLE FLOWERING.—Blooms in April, has double blossoms like roses. 50 cents.

APPLE, CHINESE DOUBLE FLOWERING.—Has clusters of double rose colored flowers, beautiful. 50c.

APPLE, DOUBLE FLOWERING WHITE.—With beautiful double white flowers; fruit a beautiful carmine. 50c. (See Fruit Department for the varieties of Crab Apples cultivated for the fruit as well as ornament.)

ASH, AMERICAN MOUNTAIN.—Similar to the European, but of a more dense habit; foliage larger with scarlet berries. 50c.

ASH, EUROPEAN MOUNTAIN.—A medium sized tree, with a graceful head, and has large clusters of showy light scarlet berries. 50c.

ASH, EUROPEAN WEEPING.—A beautiful lawn tree; rapid grower. 75c.

ASH, OAKLEAVED.—Very distinct from the former; large oak shaped leaves; fine. $1.

BEECH, AMERICAN.—Too well known to need description. Very handsome, grown in the Nursery, and desirable for Lawns, &c. $1 to $1.50.

BEECH, PURPLE LEAVED.—With dark purple foliage; beautiful. $2.

BIRCH, WHITE.—Cut Leaved Weeping; a beautiful tree, with slender drooping branches and delicately cut glossy leaves. One of the finest for ornamental purposes. $1,50 to $2.

BIRCH, WHITE.—(French,) Resembles very much the American White; upright grower and very handsome. Branches slightly pendulous. $1.

CHERRY, DOUBLE FLOWERING, LARGE.—An erect growing variety, with double blossoms. 50c.

CHERRY, DOUBLE FLOWERING, DWARF.—Similar to the preceding, only smaller. 60c.

WEEPING MOUNTAIN ASH.—See page 5.

CHERRY, LARGE WEEPING.—An imported variety, with drooping branches and black fruit. 50c.

ELM, AMERICAN—With graceful drooping branches. $1.

ELM, CAMPERDOWN.—Very distinct from the common weeping variety, being more pendulous; it forms a fine head. $2 to $3.

ELM, ENGLISH.—Very handsome, erect and lofty. $1 to $2.

HORSE CHESTNUT, WHITE FLOWERING.—Large, round, dense headed tree, with dark green foliage and large spikes of showy white and red flowers in June. 75 cts.

LABURNUM, OR GOLDEN CHAIN.—A beautiful tree, with long pendent bunches of yellow flowers. 50 cts.

LARCH, EUROPEAN.—A rapid growing pyramidal tree, with pendent branches. 75 cts.

LINDEN, AMERICAN.—(Basswood,) One of the finest of the native forest trees. $1.

MAGNOLIA, ACUMINATA.—A beautiful tree with large leaves, and yellow flowers tinted with blue. $1.

MAGNOLIA, CONSPICUA.—Cultivated in England instead of Soulangeana. $1 to $2.

MAGNOLIA, PURPUREA.—(See Ornamental Shrubs.)

MAPLE, NORWAY.—Splendid for avenues. $1.

MAPLE, SILVER LEAVED.—One of the most beautiful forest trees. $1.

MAPLE, SUGAR.—A native forest tree, of fine form and growth, with beautiful foliage. $1.

PEACH, DOUBLE FLOWERING.—Has beautiful red blossoms; one dense mass of flowers. 25 cts.

THORN, DOUBLE WHITE.—Small double white flowers. 50 cts.

THORN, PINK FLOWERING. (Rosea.)—Double flowers, fragrant. 50 cts.

TULIP TREE.—A magnificent native tree, with glossy foliage, and fiddle-shaped leaves; has tulip-like flowers and belongs to the family of Magnolias. $1.

WHITE FRINGE TREE. (Chionathus Virginica).—Handsome foliage and fine spikes of delicate white flowers. $1.

KILMARNOCK WILLOW.

WILLOW, KILMARNOCK.—A very beautiful tree, branches very pendulous, with large, glossy, dark green leaves; very hardy; worked 5 to 7 feet high on smooth stems. $1.

WILLOW, LAUREL LEAVED.—Foliage glossy dark green, like the Laurel. 75c.

WILLOW, NEW AMERICAN.—A very graceful slender branched tree, more dwarfish in its habit than the common weeping willow; grafted 5 to 7 feet high on straight, smooth stems. $1.

NEW AMERICAN WILLOW.—See page 8.

WILLOW, ROSEMARY.—A very handsome silver foliage tree, worked the same as Kilmarnock. $1.

WILLOW, WEEPING.—Too well known for description; one of the most graceful amongst trees. 50c.

Ornamental Evergreen Trees.

ARBOR VITÆ, AMERICAN OR WHITE CEDAR.—A large pyramidal tree, with deep green foliage; fine for screens or hedges. 50c.

ARBOR VITÆ, SIBERIAN.—Very hardy; retains its color during our hard winters. Very compact and upright; good for specimen lawn trees, as also for screens or hedges. 75c. to $1.

FIR, AMERICAN SILVER OR BALSAM.—A very erect pyramidal tree, with dark green foliage. 50c. to $1.

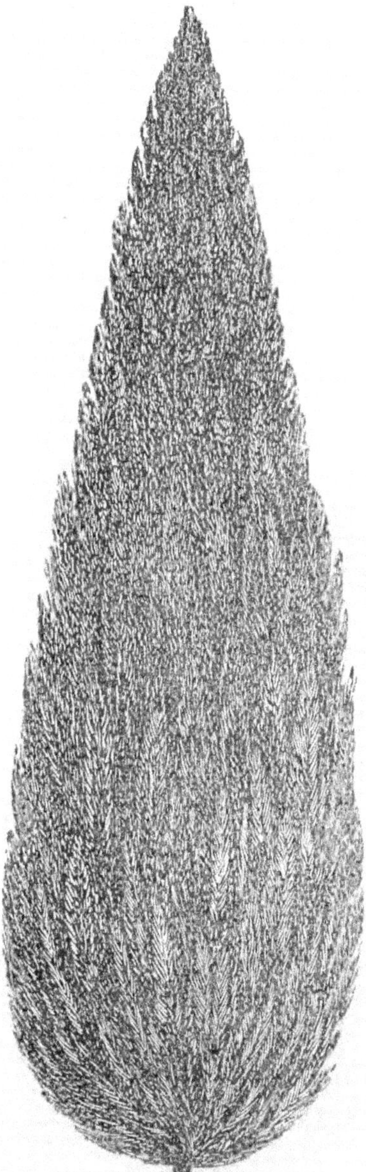

IRISH JUNIPER.

JUNIPER, ENGLISH OR COMMUNIS.—A very handsome, small, compact tree. $1.

JUNIPER, IRISH.—A very tapering, beautiful little tree. $1 to $2. (See page 10.)

JUNIPER, SWEDISH.—A small sized pyramidal tree, with bluish green foliage, very hardy and ornamental. 50 cts.

AUSTRIAN PINE.

PINE, AUSTRIAN, (Austriaca).—Black Pine; a hardy robust spreading tree; leaves long and dark green, buds large and gray, grows rapidly and is quite distinct. $1 to $1.50.

PINE, CORSICAN, (Laricio.)—A most beautiful tree, with very long leaves. $1.

PINE, SCOTCH, (Sylvestris.)—A fine, robust, rapid-growing tree, which succeeds well in this country; leaves of a silvery green. $1.

PINE, WHITE, OR WEYMOUTH, (Strobus.)—A rapid growing native Pine, with light green foliage. 50c. to $1.

SPRUCE, BLACK OR DOUBLE, (Nigra.)—Tree erect, with horizontal branches, and dark green foliage. 50c. to $1.

SPRUCE, HEMLOCK OR WEEPING.—A beautiful pyramidal tree, with drooping branches and delicate dark green foliage. 50c. to $1.

SPRUCE, NORWAY, (Excelsa.) A lofty, elegant tree, with drooping branches when it attains a medium height. 75c. to $1.

SPRUCE, WHITE AMERICAN, (Alba.)—A tapering pyramidal tree, with light bark and bluish leaves. 50c. to $1.

Evergreen Shrubs.

PRICE—25 Cents, except where noted.

BOX DWARF.—For edging; per yard, 25c.

JUNIPER, COMMON.—(See Evergreen Trees.)

JUNIPER, IRISH.—(See Evergreen Trees.)

JUNIPER, SAVIN.—A low spreading shrub.

JUNIPER, SWEDISH.—(See Evergreen Trees.)

VINCA, OR PERIWINKLE.—Running Myrtle, with dark green foliage and light blue flowers.

VINCA, VARIEGATED LEAVED.—Marked with yellow and white.

ARBOR VITÆ, (TOM THUMB.)—Very fine for low hedges and edging for drives. 25c. to 75c.

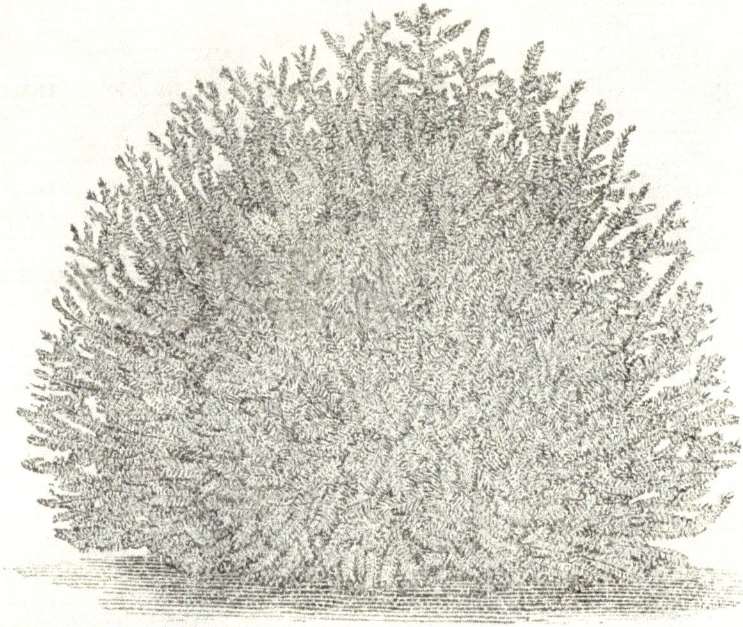

DWARF ARBOR VITÆ,—See page 12.

Ornamental Shrubs.

PRICE—25 Cents, except where noted.

ALTHEA, OR ROSE OF SHARON.—Anemone flowered. 38 cts.

" " " " " Double blue. 38 cts.

" " " " " Double red. 38 cts.

" " " " " Semi-double. 38 cts.

" " " " " Variegated-leaved. 38 cts.

All highly ornamental, and bloom profusely during the autumn.

ALMOND, DWARF DOUBLE.—Flowers like small roses.

CALYCANTHUS, ALSPICE TREE, OR SWEET SCENTED SHRUB, Wood and flowers exceedingly fragrant, of a chocolate color; very desirable. 38 cts.

CYTISUS, OR LABURNUM, TRI-FLOWERED.—A dwarf spreading shrub, with yellow flowers and quite pretty. 38 cts.

CURRANT, DOUBLE RED FLOWERING.—Beautiful.

CURRANT, SCARLET FLOWERING—Single.

CURRANT, YELLOW FLOWERING.—Bunches of sweet yellow flowers.

DEUTZIA, CRENATA FLOREPLENA.—Double white flowering. 38 cts.

DEUTZIA, CRENATE-LEAVED.—Very profuse, white flowering plant; strong grower.

DEUTZIA, GRACILIS.—Slender branched, graceful white-flowering shrub.

DEUTZIA, SCABRA.—Rough leaved Deutzia. One of the most beautiful white flowering shrubs.

EUONYMUS, STRAWBERRY TREE, OR BURNING BUSH.—A fine large shrub, bearing a profusion of scarlet berries. 38 cts.

FORSYTHEA, FORTUNII.—A new and distinct variety, with golden yellow flowers and deep green foliage.

FORSYTHEA, VIRIDISSIMA.—A deep green shrub from China; a rapid grower and free bloomer, with yellow flowers.

FRINGE TREE, PURPLE.—A much admired shrub; has curious fringed, or hair-like flowers, that cover the whole plant. Very desirable. 38 cts.

FRINGE TREE, WHITE.—(See Ornamental Trees.) $1 each.

HAWTHORNS.—(See Deciduous Trees.)

HONEYSUCKLE, UPRIGHT OR TREE, RED TARTAREAN—With red flowers.

HONEYSUCKLE, UPRIGHT OR TREE, WHITE TARTAREAN—With white flowers.

HYDRANGEA, CHANGEABLE.—An elegant plant, and very showy. 38c.

JAPAN QUINCE.—Bright red, flowering.

JAPAN QUINCE.—Deep red, flowering.

JAPAN QUINCE.—Double red, flowering.

JAPAN QUINCE.—White, flowering.

LILAC, (SYRINGA).—Common purple and white.

LILAC, CHINESE WHITE FLOWERING. 38c.

LILAC, HIMALAYENSIS.

LILAC, JOSIKÆA.—Chionanthus-leaved, purple flowering.

LILAC, PERSIAN PURPLE.—A dwarfish, round-headed, symmetrical shrub, very fragrant.

MAGNOLIA, PURPUREA.—Has large purple flowers in May and June. $1.

PRIVET, OR PRIM.—Has handsome spikes of white flowers, succeeded by black berries; makes fine hedges.

SLOE, (Prunus Trilobata.)—Double flowering plum, covered in the spring with small double pink flowers like the daisy. Very handsome. $1.

SPIREA, CALIFORNICA.—Californian.

SPIREA, CHINESE.—Has small glossy leaves and clusters of white flowers.

SPIREA, COLOSSA ALBA.—Has clusters of large white flowers.

SPIREA, CORIMBIFOLIA ALBA.—Cluster flowering; blooms the whole season.

SPIREA, CORYMBOSA.—Cluster flowering.

SPIREA, DOUBLE FLOWERING, PLUM-LEAVED.—New and beautiful. Flowers very profuse and full; blooms in May.

SPIREA, DOUGLASIIS.—Has beautiful clusters of brilliant red flowers.

SPIREA, ELM-LEAVED.—Leaves resembling those of the Elm somewhat.

SPIREA, GERMANDER-LEAVED. (Chamadafolia.)—Has small wiry branches covered with clusters of white flowers.

SPIREA, GUELDER-LEAVED.—Leaves like the snow-ball, with white flowers.

SPIREA, HOOKERII.—Hooker's.

SPIREA, HYPERICUM-LEAVED.—One mass of splendid white flowers in clusters.

SPIREA, LANCIFOLIA.—Lance-leaved.

SPIREA, REEVE'S, (Reevesii.)—A charming shrub with round head of white flowers, and narrow pointed leaves.

SPIREA, SORBUS-LEAVED.—Leaves like the mountain-ash, with spikes of flowers.

SPIREA, WHITE WILLOW-LEAVED.

SPIREA, WILLOW-LEAVED.—Long, narrow pointed leaves and rose-colored flowers.

The Spireas are all beautiful shrubs, and a long time in bloom.

SYRINGA, FRAGRANT.—(Philadelphus.)

SYRINGA, GREAT FLOWERING.—(Grandiflora.)

These are beautiful shrubs with snowy flowers in profusion.

TAMARIX.—African, German and French.

VIBURNUM, OR SNOW BALL.—A favorite well known shrub, with large globular cluster of white flowers.

VIBURNUM, HIGH BUSH CRANBERRY.—A strong growing shrub both ornamental and useful, the fruit being esteemed by many.

WEIGELIA, ALBA.—Pure white.

WEIGELIA, AMABALIS.—Pink flowered; blooms in autumn.

WEIGELIA, AMABILIS VARIEGATA.—Variegated foliage.

WEIGELIA, HORTENSIS NIVEA.

WEIGELIA, ISSOLINE.

WEIGELIA, ROSE COLORED.—A new and elegant Chinese shrub, with rose-colored flowers.

WEIGELIA, SPLENDENS.—Yellow, flowers in spring.

WEIGELIA, VAN HOUTII.

Climbing Shrubs.

Price 25 Cents.

AMPELOPSIS, OR AMERICAN IVY—Sometimes called the Virginia Creeper. A rapid grower, and attaches itself to anything it touches, like the Bignonia.

AUSTOLOCHIA.—(Dutchman's Pipe.) A fine twining plant, very large leaves, and a brownish flower shaped like a pipe. 50 cts.

BIGNONIA, OR TRUMPET FLOWER.—A splendid hardy plant, with large, scarlet, trumpet-shaped flowers.

BIGNONIA, LARGE-FLOWERED, OR CHINESE.—A more dwarf species than the former, with larger flowers and more tender. 50 cts.

GRECIAN SILK VINE.—(Periploca Græca.) A rapid twining shrub, has beautiful foliage and singular flowers; is much admired.

HONEYSUCKLE, BROWN'S. (Brownii.)—Dark foliage and scarlet flowers.

HONEYSUCKLE, CANADIAN.—A robust grower with very large glaucous leaves and yellow flowers.

HONEYSUCKLE, COMMON WOODBINE.— A robust grower and very showy; blooms in June and July.

HONEYSUCKLE, DOUGLASII.—Flowers orange-red; blooms in July and September. 50 cts.

HONEYSUCKLE, MONTHLY FRAGRANT.—Constant bloomer and very sweet.

HONEYSUCKLE, ORANGE. 50 cts.

HONEYSUCKLE, PALLIDA.—Pale flowered; white and straw-color, beautiful. 50 cts.

HONEYSUCKLE, SCARLET SUPERB.—Has longer leaves and blossoms than the following.

HONEYSUCKLE, SCARLET MONTHLY TRUMPET.—Scarlet flowers; blooms all summer.

HONEYSUCKLE, YELLOW TRUMPET.—Trumpet shaped flowers.

IVY, IRISH.—(Hibernica.) The old well-known variety. 30 cts.

WISTARIA, OR GLYCINE CHINESE.—Blue flowering. 50 cts.

The Glycine is a rapid and graceful climber, covering a large space in a single season. The flowers are in pendulous clusters, of a beautiful pale blue; bloom in June and sometimes in the fall.

Hedge Plants—Evergreen.

ARBOR VITÆ, OR WHITE CEDAR.—Transplanted and grown in Nursery rows. Stocky, fine-shaped plants.

Plants per	100	500	1000
6 to 9 inches	$4	$15	$20
12 to 15 "	7	30	45
18 to 21 "	12	50	80
2 to 2½ feet	20	90	150

ARBOR VITÆ.—(Tom Thumb.) A dwarf variety; fine for low hedges and edging for drives. Very hardy.

3 to 4 inches,	per doz.,	$2
6 "	" "	4

HEMLOCK SPRUCE.—Transplanted and grown in Nursery rows. Stocky, fine, symmetrical plants.

per	100	500	1000
6 to 9 inches,	$7	$30	$45
12 to 15 "	15	60	100
18 to 21 "	20	90	
2 to 2½ feet,	30		

NORWAY SPRUCE.—Transplanted in Nursery rows. Stocky, fine plants.

6 to 9 inches,	$10 per 100.
12 to 15 "	15 "
18 to 21	20 "
2 to 2½ feet,	25 "

DWARF BOX—For Edging, 25 cts. per yard for less than twenty-five yards. 20 cts. per yard for twenty-five yards and over.

Deciduous.

HONEY LOCUST.—Three Thorned Acacia.

One year,	$ 8 per 1000.
Two years,	12 "

JAPAN QUINCE.—A very hardy shrub-growing plant, with dark green foliage and red flowers.

1 year,	$10 per 100.
2 "	15 "
3 "	25 "

OSAGE ORANGE.—2 and 3 years $5 per 1000.

PRIVET.—Strong plants. $2 per 100, $15 per 1000.

SPIREAS.—Assorted varieties. $15 per 100.

Select Roses.

Our stock of these is very large and of the finest quality.

Miscellaneous Hardy Summer Roses.

PRICE—25 Cents; $2 per Dozen in Varieties.

AURETII.—Blackish purple; globular and double.

BELLE AFRICAINE.—Full, double; very dark indeed.

BELLE PARABERE.—Purplish violet.

BIZARRE DE LA CHINA.—Crimson purple, large and double.

BLANCHE FLEUR.—Pure White;—blooms in large clusters.

BONNE GENEVEIVE.—Purple and crimson, globular and double.

CELINE.—Rose cupped, very large and fine.

CERICETTE.—Beautiful bright red, very double.

CHENEDOLLE.—Very large, double and fragrant; light crimson.

CLAIRE D'OLIBAN.—Delicate rose.

COMMON PROVENCE.—Rose color; large, double and fragrant.

CRAMOISI PICOTE.—Crimson violet; finally spotted.

DOCTOR BILLARD.—Vivid scarlet, showy.

DUC D'ENGHIEN.—Incarnate.

DUKE OF ORLEANS.—Bright rose, spotted with white; large.

DUKE OF SUSSEX.—Pale rose, center, ruby velvet. Very fine.

ERNEST FERRAY.—Light rose.

FLORA McIVOR.—Rosy lilac, superb.

GENERAL BERNARD.—Purple, shaded with crimson.

GEORGE IV.—Crimson velvet, dark; large and double.

GEORGE VIBERT.—Medium, full; violet red, streaked with white.

GRAND HUBERT.—Full, double rose.

ISABELLE DE LORAINE.—Rose, edged, and spotted, large.

JULIETTE—Bright rose, outside petals white.

LOUIS PHILLIPPE.—Crimson and carmine.

LUXEMBOURG.—Rosy lilac, edged with rose.

MADAME PLANTIER.—One of the finest white roses; cupped, double, and blooms profusely.

NARCISSE DE SALVANDY.—Purple, bordered with white.

ŒILLET FLAMMAND.—Striped with white.

ŒILLET PARFAIT.—Red, striped with white, like a carnation.

PARIGOT.—Brilliant crimson, cupped and double.

PERFECTA.—Most splendid, beautiful light pink.

PERLE DES PANCHES.—Medium size, white, striped with violet, double

PONIATOWSKI.—Rose, shaded with lilac.

POURPRE.—Purplish rose, large and full.

PRINCE NORMAND.—Blush.

PRINCESSE DE SIAM.—Reddish carmine, shaded with violet; globular.

REINE DE FRANCAIS.—Most splendid silvery blush; one of the very best.

RICHELIEU.—Rosy lilac, fine.

ROI DE PRUSSIA.—Dark, coronet in center.

VIOLETTE BILLARD.—Reddish violet, edged with deeper violet.

Moss Roses.

Price—38 Cents; $3 per dozen.

ADELAIDE.—Double, expanded and perfect form, blush; very vigorous grower.

A FEUILLES LUISANTES.—Rose, full and double.

ALICE LE ROY.—Lilac, rose, large and full.

BOURSIER DE LA RIVIERE.—Large and full, cupped, very fine form; bright deep red, moss very dark, in clusters.

CAPT. JOHN INGRAHAM.—Full, dark purple, velvet.

CATHARINE DE WURTEMBERG.—Rose, double, vigorous habit.

CELINA.—Brilliant crimson, large glossy foliage.

COUNTESS DE MURINAIS.—Pure white, in clusters; large and double.

CRESTED MOSS.—Rose color; buds curiously crested.

CRIMSON.—(Common Pink.) Double, bright crimson; very mossy.

DIAPHANE.—Full rose, anemone form.

DIDON.—Light rose color.

ELIZABETH ROW.—Pale rose, spotted with white.

ETNA.—Purplish flame color; superb.

JEAN BODIN.—Full, globulous, extra form; very beautiful and superb.

JEANNE DE MONTFORT.—Large and full, rosy flesh color; in clusters.

JENNY LIND.—A most superb rose, justly entitled to the name of Queen of Mosses. The branches, peduncle, petals, seed receptacle, and the calyx are all covered with a very thick, beautiful, reddish colored moss.

LANE.—Very large and full, rosy violet, changing to lilac.

LATONE.—Very large and full, delicate rose, approaching carmine.

LOUISE COLLET.—Pale rose, with curious leafy calyx.

LUXEMBOURG.—Large, cupped, fine purplish crimson; luxuriant grower and fine bloomer.

MARIE DE BLOIS.—Very large and full, clear rosy satin.

NUIT DE YOUNG.—Full, deep purple maroon, velvet.

OCTAVIE.—Pale rosy lilac, large and full.

PARMENTIER.—Large, double, reddish purple.

POMPON D'ANGERS.—Small, double-purple, rose.

PRECOCE.—Full, clear, rosy crimson.

WILLIAM LOBB.—Very double, blooms in clusters; carmine shaded into violet.

ZAIRBINE.—Full, deep rose.

Perpetual Moss Roses.

Price, 38 Cents, except where noted.

ALFRED DE DALMAS.—Rosy center, edges white, blooms in clusters, very double.

CELINE BRIANT.—Deep rose, blooms in clusters.

DELPHINE.—Full brilliant rose.

DELILLE.—Medium, full, lively red. 50 cts.

HERMAN KEGEL.—Double, crimson violet, white striped; the best Moss known. 50 cts.

MADAME EDOUARD ORY.—Large, full, beautiful rosy carmine. 50 cts.

MARIE DE BOURGOGNE.—Middle size, full rose color. 50 cts.

OSCAR LE CLERC.—Full, rosy lilac, spotted with white.

PERPETUAL WHITE.—Pure white, often with a pink stripe, large clusters and vigorous grower, very mossy.

POMPON PERPETUELLE.—Small, full, rose, lilac.

SALET.—Large and full, bright rose, passing to pale rose.

Climbing Roses.

Price, 25 Cents. $2 per dozen.

This list comprises all the running Roses, fine for trellises, walls and screens. They are hardy, rapid growers, with luxuriant foliage, bearing immense clusters of beautiful flowers, of all shades; and like the Kentucky Multiflora, continue their blooming to a very late period.

Multiflora Roses.

GREVILLE, OR SEVEN SISTERS.—Varying from white to purple. Blooms in large clusters.

KENTUCKY MULTIFLORA, OR MOUNT JOY.—Splendid double rose, in clusters, creamy white.

Double Michigan, or Prairie Roses.

Price—25 Cents each; $2 per dozen.

ANNA MARIA.—Pink, with rosy center, cupped, full, double, beautiful large clusters of 20 to 30 flowers quite distinct.

BALTIMORE BELLE.—Pale blush, nearly white, full and double in large clusters; rapid grower and very fragrant.

BEAUTY, OR QUEEN OF PRAIRIES.—Bright rosy red, with a white stripe in the center of each petal; very large and globular. An immense bloomer.

EVA CORRINNE.—Very delicate blush with beautiful center, globular and very double, 10 to 20 flowers in a cluster, and quite fragrant; very desirable.

GEM OF THE PRAIRIES.—Light shade of crimson, blotched with white.

JANE.—Lilac rose, imbricated and very double; clusters large, 25 to 30 flowers in each. Very robust.

LINNÆAN HILL BEAUTY.—Pale blush, very fine, and much admired; clusters large and full.

MISS GUNNELL.—Elegant, delicate blush or buff; clusters from 25 to 30 flowers. One of the best.

MRS. HOVEY.—Splendid blush and beautiful clusters, large, of superb habit, and splendid deep foliage. Parsons says, sometimes pure white.

MRS. PIERCE.—White.

PERPETUAL PINK.—Deep pink changing to purple, blooms sometimes in Autumn.

PRESIDENT.—Blush, with rosette in the center, compact, vigorous, 15 to 20 flowers in a cluster.

PRIDE OF WASHINGTON.—Very dark rose, fine form, cupped, resembling Jane, vigorous, clusters of about 20 flowers.

RANUNCULIFLORA.—Pale blush, very handsome, large clusters of about 25 to 30 flowers, foliage large and deeply serrated; a remarkable variety.

TRIUMPHANT.—Deep brilliant rose, imbricated; clusters large, 20 to 30 flowers, foliage large and deeply serrated; a remarkable variety.

VIRGINIA LASS.—Splendid blush, in large clusters.

Perpetual, or Ever-Blooming Roses.

This is the most desirable class of all the Roses, being mostly hardy, and having the quality of blooming during the full season. They are of vigorous growth, fine foliage, and rich in their colors; ranging from pure white to deep brilliant scarlet, and even to very dark purple, or almost black.

PRICE—38 Cents each, except where noted.

" By the doz., selections mainly left to us, $3.

ABRAHAM LINCOLN.—New, dark purple, large, full, fine form, free flowering, vigorous grower. 75 cts.

DELE MAUZE.—Rose color with blue tinge, fine.

ALBA CARNEA.—New, white, lightly tinged with rose flowers; medium, good grower. 75 cts.

ANNIE GIBBON.—Brilliant rose, very sweet.

ANGELINA GRANGER.—Large and full rose, fine formed.

ANTIGONE.—Deep, changing to light rose; large.

ARICIE.—Bright rose, large globose.

ARTHUR DE SANSEL.—Very full, dark purple, tinged with fiery red.

AUBERNON.—Brilliant rose, very fragrant.

AUGUSTE MIE.—Pink, carmine centre, large and full, very showy.

AUGUSTINE MOUCHELET.—Deep, purplish red; blooms in clusters, large and full.

BARON LARREY.—Rosy carmine, large and full.

BARON PREVOST.—Deep rose, large and full, superb.

BARRONNE HALLER DE'CLAPAREDE—Full, brilliant carmine, most splendid, very rare and beautiful. A seedling of Madame Laffay, elegant foliage, flowers larger, more double, and petals much thicker.

BELLE D'ORLEANS.—Large and full; bright satin rose.

BEAUTY OF WATTHAM.—Bright crimson, one of the best.

BERANGER.—Large, full, globular, purplish crimson; very fine.

CALARDEAUX.—Dark purple, very fine.

CAPTAIN JOHN FRANKLIN.—Large, full, rosy carmine, fine.

CAROLINE DE SANSEL.—Centre large and full, as Baron Prevost; very fine.

CELINA DUBOIS, OR BLANCHE DU ROI.—Light flesh color, changing to pure white, sometimes tinted with rose; very fine.

CHARLES VERDIER.—New, rose color, edge of petals whitish, large, full smooth; strong growth. 75 cts.

CHARLES ROULARD.—Bright rose, full and perfect; extra.

CHARLES VIRDIER.—Fine rose color, edges large and full, petals whitish; extra.

COMTE DE ROBINSKY.—A remarkable rose, brighter in color than Geant des Battailles; nearly scarlet.

COMTE DE DERBY.—Bright rose, large and full, very vigorous and fine.

COURONNE DE BERANGER.—A purplish crimson rose, distinct, large and full, one of the best.

DIEUL DE PRINCE ALBERT.—Purplish crimson, very dark, velvety, very full; shy bloomer.

DR. ARNUL.—(Margottin.) Bright red, large and fine.

DR. HENON.—Medium, full, globular, pure white, with center yellowish.

DR LINDLEY.—Bright red, with purple center, large and fine.

DR. MARX.—Rosy carmine, full and large.

DR. REYNAUD.—Large size, full, spotted rose, superb.

DUC D'ALENCON.—Lilac rose, profuse bloomer, large and full.

DUC D'AUMALE.—Bright crimson, cupped, fragrant.

DUC NEMOURS.—Pale delicate rose, very full and double.

DUCHESS DE PRASLIN.—Very full, petal inside clear rose, outside pure white.

EARL TALBOT.—Large, deep clear rose.

EDWARD JESSE.—Lilac rose, large and beautiful.

EMPEROR NAPOLEON III.—Large and full, bright crimson rose, shaded to dark brown violet.

ETENDARD OF MARENGO.—A most beautiful brilliant crimson variety, of the most perfect form and worthy of a place in the most limited collection.

EUGENE SCRIBE.—New, bright dazzling red, and full; growth strong. 75 cts.

EUGENE SUE.—Large, double, globular, equal to Baron Prevost, lively rose color, very fragrant.

FELIX GENERO.—New, beautiful rose, shaded with violet, perfect form, good grower. $1.

GEANT DE BATTAILLES, (Giant of battles.)—Brilliant crimson, full and double.

GEN. DELANGE.—Light rose, large and fine.

GEN. JACQUEMINOT.—Large size, full, bright red, very showy, fine grower.

GEN. SIMPSON.—Carmine, finely formed, good bloomer.

GENIE DE CHATEAUBRIAND.—A great rose, crimson amaranth, shaded with black.

GUILBERT SLATER.—Very full, splendid clear purple.

HORACE VERNET.—New, velvety reddish purple, shaded with deep crimson; flowers large. $1.

JACQUES LAFITTE.—Rosy carmine, with a light edge; very sweet.

JULES MARGOTTIN.—Bright cherry, large and full; superb.

LADY FORDWICK.—Deep rose, full and double; in large clusters.

LA RANUNCULE.—Bright red, ranunculus form, fragrant.

LA REINE.—Deep rosy lilac, superb, very large.

L' ENFANT DU MONT CARMEL.—Purplish red, large and full.

LEONIDE LE ROI.—Flesh color, full and double, fine clusters.

LILACEA.—Delicate rosy lilac, large, vigorous grower.

LION OF COMBATS.—Crimson scarlet, brilliant and showy.

LOUISE LE CLERC THOUIN.—Another of the very finest roses, of splendid form, full petals, on the inside beautiful incarnate, outside beautiful rose color.

MADAME AIMEE.—Rose incarnate, beautiful.

MADAME ALFRED ROUGEMONT.—White, slightly shaded carmine.

MADAME ANDRY.—Rosy violet, cupped.

MADAME CORNET.—Delicate rose, large and full, free grower.

MADAME EUGENE CAVAIGNAC.—Large, very double globular, delicate rose.

MADAME FREEMAN.—White, cupped, medium size.

MADAME FLORY.—Rosy lilac, shaded white, very sweet, large, full and imbricated; worthy a place in every collection.

MADAME GEORGE PAUL.—New, beautiful shaded and tinted rose with whitish edges, large flowers. $1.

MADAME GUILLOT.—A beautiful rosy crimson, with very double flowers; has attained a great reputation in England.

MADAME HECTOR JACQUIN.—Clear, rose, shaded with lilac, large and full.

MADAME HILAIRE.—Very fine, beautiful rosy lilac.

MADAME LAFFAY.—Rosy, crimson, large, full, superb.

MADAME PEUPIN OR PEPIN.—Soft rose color, flowers large and full, the back of the petal almost white; a very beautiful rose.

MADAME RIVAL.—New, delicate satiny rose, large, double and well formed.

MADAME TRUDEAUX.—Large, full, bright crimson, fine bloomer.

MADAME VIDOT.—Large and full, fine form, white, tinted with rose.

MD'LLE ANNIE WOOD.—New, clear red, finely imbricated, large and full.

MD'LLE JEANNE MARIX.—New, bright rose, shaded with purple, large and full.

MARCHAL VAILLIANT.—Bright, reddish purple, strong grower, large and full.

MARGUERITE D'ANJOU.—A most splendid rose, fine form, with stained appearance.

MARIA BERNARDIERE.—Rosy lilac, very large, good bloomer.

MARQUIS DE BOCELLA.—Delicate, rosy blush, full and perfect, blooming nearly white.

MELANIE CORNU.—Deep, reddish violet, full and double.

MOGADOR, OR POURTRE ROSE DU ROI.—Deep purplish red.

MONSIEUR PLAISANCON.—New, deep carmine, flowers large and cupped; strong grower. $1.

MONTAIGNE.—Fine deep rose.

MRS. ELLIOT.—Rich rosy purple, large and full.

MRS. RIVERS.—Large, globular, lilac, very handsome.

NAOMI.—Splendid blush, with a rose center, superb.

NAPOLEON III.—New, brilliant scarlet and violet, fine and distinct; one of the best. $1.

OLINER DE SERRES.—Large and full deep rose, curious foliage.

PÆONIA.—Large and full, rosy crimson, fine.

PALAIS DE CRYSTAL.—Splendid flesh color, very large, double and imbricated, with somewhat of a copper colored center.

PANACHE D'ORLEANS.—Full, well, formed, striped with bright carmine superb.

PAUL VERDIER.—New, very bright rose color, large, full, and imbricated; good grower. $1.

PIE IX.—Full, beautiful form crimson violet, one of the handsomest.

PORTLAND BLANC.—Very large, fine and full, pure white.

PRINCE ALBERT.—Rose, changing to violet, large and fine.

PRINCE NOIR.—Very dark purplish crimson, double fine.

PRUDHOMME.—Bright rose in clusters.

REINE DE LA GUILLOTINE.—Dark crimson, full and fine.

REINE MATHILDE.—Well worthy of cultivation, if only for its color, which is of the freshest, softest pink; flowers very constantly.

RIVERS' CRIMSON.—Brilliant rosy crimson, large and full.

ROSE PERFECTION.—New, deep rose color, form perfect, large and full. $1.

ROSINE MARGOTTIN.—Large, full, imbricated, clear rose, most beautiful.

SOUVENIR DE LA REINE D'ANGLETERRE.—Large and full, bright shaded rose.

SOUVENIR DE MONS BOLL.—New, reddish cerise, rich shaded, large and well formed. $1.

SOUVENIR LEVISON GOWER.—Bright dazzling carmine, very large and double.

SYDONIE.—Light pink, very large and full.

THORIN.—New, beautiful pure rose color, fine form, and large. $1.

TRIOMPHE DE L'EXPOSITION.—Very large and full, bright rosy, crimson.

TRIOMPHE DE PARIS.—Large and full, deep red velvet.

VICTORIA, (Paul.)—Nearly white, as large and double as La Reine; one of the best light-colored Perpetuals out.

VICTOIRE D'AUSTERLITZ.—Most delicate pink.

VOLTA.—Very large and full, cupped, showy rose.

WILLIAM JESSE.—Rosy crimson, very large and full.

WILLIAM GRIFFITH.—Superb, glossy rose, of most perfect form.

YOLAND D'ARAGON.—Rosy blush; in large clusters.

Yellow ,or Austrian Roses.

38 Cents each.

AUSTRIAN YELLOW.—Single, bright yellow.

HARRISON'S DOUBLE YELLOW.—Double, bright yellow, and very free bloomer.

PERSIAN YELLOW.—Deep golden yellow, large and double; good bloomer.

[These are very hardy and distinct.]

Bourbon Roses.

PRICE—38 Cents each, except where noted.
" By the doz., chiefly our selection, $3.

The Bourbons, as a class, are more tender than the Perpetuals; but are vigorous growers, continual bloomers, and fine in foliage. They bloom in large clusters and are very lasting. Their best season is in the autumn, when fine roses are most desirable. We ask attention to the collection below, as embracing not only the very rare and choice new varieties imported during recent years, but also all the best varieties heretofore for sale in our country.

We are also constantly importing from abroad, and shall spare no pains to keep well supplied with the latest and choicest varieties.

ANAIS.—Bright rose.

ANN BELUZE.—Blush white, or incarnate, superb.

APPOLINE.—A pretty, delicate shaded rose.

AURORE DU GUIDE.—Bright dazzling red, changing to clear violet.

BEAUTE LYONNAISE.—Large, full, imbricated, perfect rosy lilac.

BEAUTE DE VERSAILLES.—Full, brilliant rose.

CARDINAL FESH.—Violet crimson, very double.

CESARINE SOUCHET.—Large and full, fine, delicate rose, edged with bright rose.

COMTE DE RAEBUTEAU.—Full, clear red, changing to violet.

DOCTOR ROQUES.—Purplish crimson, fine.

DUCHESS DE NORMANDIE.—Full, bright rose, very double.

DUC DE CHARTRAS.—Large, double, crimson.

EDWARD DESFOSSES.—Deep, rosy pink, large and full; fine.

EMPRESS EUGENIE.—Blush white or incarnate, large and full.

FERDINAND DEPPE.—Full, velvety, rosy amaranth.

GEORGE CUVIER.—Beautiful cherry.

GUILLIAUME LE CONQUERANT.—Large and full, brilliant rose.

HERMOSA.—Light blush, full and double, fine.

JULIA DE FONTENELLE.—Crimson violet, fine.

JUPITER.—Deep violet crimson, beautiful.

LADY CANNING.—Rosy lilac, large and full.

LEVISION GOWER.—Deep rose, large and full.

LOUISE ODIER.—Double, flame color, very brilliant, form very perfect.

LOUISE MARGOTTIN.—Glossy, transparent rose.

MADAME DESPRES.—Rosy lilac, large and full.

MADAME FONTAINE.—Large and full, rich crimson velvet.

MADAME NERARD.—Full, delicate flesh color.

MADAME VARENGOT.—Full, violet red, superb.

MARQUISE DE MOYRIA.—Large, full, brilliant rose.

MARQUISE DE BALBIANO.—Large and full, fine form, rosy carmine.

MONTHLY CABBAGE.—Bright rose, very fine.

OMER PACHA.—Full, imbricated, brilliant scarlet, passing to carmine.

PAUL JOSEPH.—Deep purple, rich and beautiful.

PAXTON.—Large and full, bright rosy pink; flowers, finished in the most dainty perfection; blooms in clusters.

PREMICES DE PONTOISE.—Medium size, flesh color, full.

PREMIBES DES CHARPENNES.—Satin rose, clouded and imbricated, fine.

PRINCE DE SALM.—Very fine purple.

PRINCESS CLEMENTINE.—Purple, shaded with crimson.

QUEEN OF BOURBONS.—Delicate fawn color, very fragrant.

SOUVENIR DE LA MALMAISON.—Incarnate, large, very double and fine; much admired.

Musk Scented Roses.

HERBEMON CLUSTER.—Blush; flowers in large clusters; free bloomer. Price 25 cents.

Noisettes.

The Noisettes are a splendid class of roses, and are justly admired by all.

PRICE—38 Cents, except where noted.

" per dozen, our selection mainly, $3.

ALBA.—Medium flower, pale flesh, changing to white, very free bloomer, beautiful.

AMI VIBERT.—Pure white, blooms in clusters; one of the hardiest.

AUGUSTA.—This rose has proved itself to be the finest of Noisettes, a very vigorous grower, with splendid foliage, and of the most free blooming habit. The flowers are of a fine yellow and deliciously fragrant; form globular and perfect. 75c.

Strong two year old plants on their own roots, $1.50.

CAROLINE MARNIESSE.—Full, white incarnate; ranks in England as one of the best.

CHROMATELLA.—Deep yellow, large and beautiful.

CLARA WENDEL.—Aurora, changing to straw color.

EUDOXIE.—Full and globular, light yellowish flesh.

EUPHROSINE.—Pale rose and yellow; great bloomer, very sweet, large and very double.

FELLEMBERG.—Brilliant crimson; large and full.

FRANKLIANA.—Very full; white and fragrant.

FLEUR D'AGE.—Large, yellow tinged with pink; very fragrant.

JACQUES AMYOT.—Flowers large, beautiful rosy lilac, very fine bloomer.

JEANE SOUFRE MUSCAT.—Creamy yellow, and very sweet.

LAMARQUE.—Pale lemon yellow, large and fine.

MADAME DES LONGCHAMPS.—Rosy white, finely formed, small and double.

MARSHAL NEIL.—Rich canary yellow, vigorous grower, monthly bloomer and free flowerer; one of the best. $1.

MORPHEE.—Rose, petals pointed, unique.

OCTAVIE.—Fine reddish purple, extra.

OPHIRE.—Bright salmon or fawn; fine.

PHALÆ.—Large, full, white, shaded with rose; superb.

SOLFATARE.—Saffron yellow, large and fine.

VITELLINA.—White, with a yellowish rosy center; very pretty and fine.

WOODLAND MARGUERITE.—Pure white.

China, or Bengal Roses.

This class is desirable and fine for the open ground, filling up the entire season with a profusion of bloom. In their habit they are comparatively dwarfish. They commence flowering in April, and continue a constant succession until arrested by frost. If potted and housed, they will continue to bloom throughout the winter months. They are all tender, and require protection.

PRICE—38 Cents, except where noted.
" $3 per dozen, our selection.

AGRIPPINA.—Rich velvety crimson.

AIME DESPRES.—Small, double, rosy violet.

CARMINE ROYAL.—Deep carmine; beautiful.

CELS.—Blush, large and profuse bloomer.

EUGENE PEROL.—Rosy crimson; free bloomer.

HENRI PLANTIER.—Bright red; good bloomer.

INDICA SUPERBA—Deep rose, large.

JETEROSE.—Creamy white.

LOUIS PHILLIPPE.—Rich dark crimson.

PINK DAILY.—Profuse bloomer, pink.

PRINCE CHARLES.—Bright carmine.

PRINCE EUGENE.—Dark rose color; free bloomer.

PURPLE CROWN.—Splendid dark rose.

SANGUINEA.—Dark red, white stripe.

VIRGINALE.—Light flesh; beautiful.

WHITE DAILY.—Pure white; great bloomer.

Tea Roses.

These Roses are particularly esteemed on account of their exquisite odor, denominated tea-scented.

PRICE—38 Cents, except where noted.
" per dozen, our selection, $3.

ADAM.—Brilliant pink.

AMONEA.—Light flesh, very beautiful.

CLARA SYLVAIN.—Pure white; superb.

DOCT. KANE.—Yellow.

ELIZA SAUVAGE.—Pale, yellow, orange center.

GEN. TARTAS.—Large, full, deep rose.

GREEN ROSE.—Flowers entirely green; a curiosity.

LA SYLPHIDE.—Rosy buff, large and beautiful.

LADY WARRENDER.—Pure white with creamy center; very fine.

LAONTINE LAPORTE.—Large and full, yellow, tinged with buff.

LE PACTOLE.—Pale lemon yellow; very fine.

LYONNAIS.—Pale flesh color, cupped.

MADAME DE SALVANDY.—Large, yellow, changing to buff; remarkably fine.

MADAME MARGOTTIN.—New, beautiful citron yellow; center rosy peach, edge of petals white; large and double. $1.

MERLE DE LABULAIS.—Cream color, edged with rose; cupped.

NEPHOTOS.—Large and globular, pale yellow, fine.

ODORATISSIMA.—Blush, with deeper center; fine.

PRINCESSE HELEN MODESTE.—Blush white, fine.

PRINCESSE MARIE.—Rosy blush; large.

SIR WALTER SCOTT.—Pale rose color, very fine.

SOUVENIR D'UN AMI.—Large, full pale rose; one of the best.

SOUVENIR 30TH MAY.—Most beautiful soft or light rose, flower large and very fine.

TAGLIONI.—Creamy white, large and fine.

TRIOMPHE DE LUXEMBOURG.—Large aurora, shaded pink; very fine and much esteemed.

VICTORIA MODESTE.—Blush pink.

VICOMTESSE DE CAZES.—Yellow, shaded with copper.

WILLIAM WALLACE.—Pale blush.

ZEPHYRINE.—Pale yellow; fine.

Banksia Roses.

PRICE—38 Cents each.

WHITE.—Pure white, small, very double and pretty, in large clusters.

YELLOW.—Similar to the preceding, with clear yellow flowers.

Phloxes.

The Phloxes are at this time the most popular of all herbaceous perennials. They are very easy of culture, and being unbounded bloomers, they emblazon the early autumn with a lavish profusion of the most exquisite colors. Our collection comprises the very best old and new varieties. Whole roots may be had in the fall and spring; also plants in pots in the spring, suitable for bedding out for early fall blooming.

PRICE—Unless otherwise noted, 18 Cents each; per doz., $1.50.

BEAUTY SUPREME.—Rose, carmine center.

COUNTESS OF MORTON.—White, fine form.

DECORA.—White, violet eye, very delicate; dwarf habit.

EMPEREUR DE RUSSIA.—Violet shaded, purple center.

GABRIEL.—Cherry, with dark throat.

GRAND SULTAN.—Pure white, carmine center; extra fine.

HARRISONII.—Clear white.

HENRY LIERVAL.—Purple, very dark; the best of its color.

IMPERIALIS.—White, bright carmine center.

LA VOLUPTE.—Glazed pink, lilac center.

LOUIS GERMAIN.—Pink, with rich purple center; dwarfish.

MADAME D'ARGENT.—Pale rose, crimson eye.

MADAME FERRAND.

MADAME LIERVAL.—Velvety carmine, flowering in large clusters; small eye.

MA'MOISELLE JUDITH.—White, rosy center, shaded purple.

MAXIMILIAN.—Dwarf, veined rose, with reddish center.

McSERRIE.—White, with bright pink center.

MONSIEUR FORGET.—Reddish purple, very large.

MRS. BUIST.—Large, pure white, fine form and habit.

MRS. MORCEAU.—Dark purple red, very showy and fine.

NEPTUNE.—Rosy carmine, beautiful.

PRESIDENT DECAINSE.—Bright carmine, good habit.

ROI DE LEOPOLD.—Large, lilac white.

SOUVENIR 29TH OCT.—Pure white, rosy lilac center, dwarfish habit; one of the best.

STRIATA SUPERBA.—White striped, rosy lilac.

VICTOR HUGO.—Rich rosy carmine.

Pæonies.—Tree Pæonies.

PRICE—$2 to $4 each.

A good Collection.

These shrubby bushes, from three to five feet in height, when covered in the month of May with their large, showy, and beautiful flowers, are highly attractive; and even a small collection of shrubbery cannot be complete without them.

Herbaceous Pæonies.

PRICE—30 Cents each, except otherwise noted.

" per dozen, $2.50; $16 per 100.

The Herbaceous Pæonies are very beautiful and showy, and deserve a place in even the smallest garden. A selection can be made which will bloom nearly three months.

ALBICANS PLENA.—Double, rosy pink, changing to white; hangs on a long time.

AMABILIS GRANDIFLORA.—Outside flesh color, center delicate straw, large and fine.

ANEMONE FLORA ALBA.—Outer petals very large, of a fine white, center ones narrow, of a creamy yellow; stigma rose colored.

ANEMONE STRIATA.—Outer petals very large, rosy violet; center ones small, rose and salmon, centers elevated, fine.

BICOLOR.—Yellowish white, center marked with carmine. 50c.

BICOLOR TRIUMPHANS.—Outer petals large, pink; center rich straw color; often in clusters.

CENTRIPETALLA ROSEA ALBA.—Very double, rose colored.

EDULIS ALBA.—Center petals blush fading to white; center light straw; stigma colored. 50c.

EDULIS SUPERBA.—Beautiful rose, lightly shaded with violet, with whitish lines, flowers globular; a superb variety.

ELEGANS.—Large, light blush, almost white, center yellowish, stigma carmine.

ELEGANS, SUPERBISSIMA.—Very large and double, center petals white and fringed, outer ones pink, stigma colored.

ELEGANTISSIMA.—Outside blush, inside yellow, anemone flowered.

ENDLIS.—Violet rose. 50c.

FESTIVA.—Flowers large, pure white, tipped with carmine, form exquisite, globular and full; this is the most magnificent of all. 50c.

FORMOSA.—Yellowish white, stigma bright rose; large, full and globular, a fine variety, beautiful. 50c.

HUMEII.—Immensely large, deep pink, full double, rose formed, scentless.

LATIPETALLA ROSEA ALBA.—Outer petals light pink, center full white, very beautiful.

LILACINA PLENISSIMA.—White, very large and double, outer petals blush, fading to white.

MAIDEN'S BLUSH SUPERB.—Very large, fine blush, stigma rose colored. 50c.

NIVALIS.—Pure white, outer petals small and fringed, very large, in clusters; splendid. 50c.

PERFECTA.—White, occasionally a petal edged with rich purple crimson, large, very full double, and rose scented.

PLENISSIMA ROSEA FLORA PLENA.—Pink, very large, full, double, outer petals very broad and handsome. 50c.

PLENISSIMA ROSEA SUPERBA.—Flowers large, double and full, beautiful rose, superb.

PLENISSIMA ROSEA VARIEGATA.—Pink, very double and handsome.

POTTSII.—Immensely large, full, double, dark purple, sweet scented, magnificent. 50c.

PROLIFERA TRICOLOR.—Outer petals clear blush, center straw color, stigma purple; a beautiful variety.

QUEEN VICTORIA.—Outer petals large, white, shaded slightly with rose, center yellowish and fringed, stigma purple; superb and sweet.

REVESII.—Delicate rose, with purple fringed petals, very large, sweet scented. 50c.

ROSEA ALBA LUTESCENS.—White center, petals long, pointed and quilled; very pretty.

ROSEA FRAGRANS.—Double, rose colored and fragrant; very fine.

ROSEA SPECIOSA.—Very large and full, pink fading to white, center petals fringed. 50c.

RUBRA.—Large double crimson, magnificent.

SINENSIS ALBA FLORA PLENA.—White, very large, full double, stigma pink; very handsome.

SINENSIS EDULIS FLORA PLENA.—Large, full double, rich flake rare and beautiful; rose-scented.

SINGLE RED.—As its name imports.

TRICOLOR GRANDIFLORA PLENA.—Very large and full, light blush, center full and feathered, stigma rose.

VENUSTISSIMA.—Large, delicate blush fading to white, petals splashed or feathered; fine.

VICTORIA MODESTE.—Outer petals beautiful rosy violet, center ones lined with a salmon stripe, large, double and full.

VICTORIA TRICOLOR.—Outer petals pale rose, mottled with pink, center yellowish white, often edged with purple, very large and full.

WHITTLEJI.—White center, slightly yellowish, very large and sweet; in clusters.

Also the following choice varieties:

LOUIS VAN HOTTE.—Dark crimson. 50c.

PIO NONO. 50c.

POTTSII FOLIO ELEGANTE, VARIEGATED. 50c.

QUEEN PERFECTA.—Black white. 50c.

REINE HORTENSE. 50c.

SPECIOSA STRIATA.—Rose, whitish center. 50c.

TENUIFOLIA FLORA PLENA. 50c.

VERSICOLOR EXTRA. 50c.

WITTMANII.—Pearly white, yellow center. 50c.

Chrysanthemums.

The fall can boast of no flower more beautiful than the Chrysanthemums. They are a great ornament to parlor windows, and make the green house look gay until Christmas. Many of the large flowering varieties are very handsome and showy; but the introduction of the Pompone or Daisy varieties, which are of a dwarf or compact habit and more adapted to pot culture, has nearly monopolized public attention and favor. They flower in all shades of color, being very neat in their appearance, many resembling a most perfect Daisy. The following list comprises the best French and other varieties. The largest flowering varieties are marked by a star. *

Dwarf or Pompone Chrysanthemums.

PRICE—30 Cents each. Per doz., $3.

*ALFRED SALTER.—Rosy lilac, very large and full. Extra.

*ALPHONSE BOISDUVAL.—Copper color, large.

BELOT DE BOUGERES.—Light crimson, yellow center.

CANARY BIRD—Yellow.

CHEDEVILLE.—Yellow and brown, very handsome.

COMPTE DE CHAMBORD.—White, straw center.

FAIRY NYMPH.—Pure white, free, early bloomer.

FRANCOISE.—Light blush.

*GLOIRE DE MONT ROUGE.—Yellow and red.

GOLDEN HERMINE.—Golden yellow.

GRAND NAPOLEON.—Dark crimson.

IPHEGENIA.—Light rose, extra.

LA BIZARRE.—White, brown center.

LADY HARDING.—Rose pink.

LAIS.—Pink.

MADAME SCHMIDT.—Flesh, with purple center; fine.

MARTRICARIOIDES.—Small and very neat, color mulberry.

MISS LANE.—Orange and red.

MONSIEUR PEPIN.—Mahogany red.

PERFECTA.—Beautiful pink, imbricated.

REINE D'OR.—Pink yellow center.

ROI DE LILLIPUT.—Brilliant red, lemon center.

ROSE D'AMOUR.—Rose, richly shaded.

SACRAMENT.—Orange yellow.

SNOW FLAKE.—White.

SOLFATARE.—Beautiful yellow.

SURPRISE.—White, striped with pink; splendid.

TACITE.—White, with yellow center.

TEMPLE OF SOLOMON.—Deep yellow.

VELEDA.—Beautiful white, lemon center, double; fine.

VIRGINIA QUEEN.—Snow white, neat habit.

WARDEN.—Mahogany Red.

YELLOW KING.—Golden yellow.

Carnations and Picotees.

The beauty and brilliancy of the flowers of the Carnation and Picotee, together with their delicious fragrance, cause them to be not only very popular but to have many ardent admirers.

PRICES.—Finest named sorts, each 30 cts.; per doz., $3.

AMY ROBSART.—Purple edged.

BLACK PRINCE.—Deep maroon.

BONFIRE.—Flaming bright red, dashed with crimson; large and fine.

EMPEROR.—Yellow, with rosy scarlet margin.

GENERAL TAYLOR.—Crimson on bizarre.

IVANHOE.—Purple.

LA FLORIFERE.—White, rose mottled; extra.

M'LLE VERNAY.—White, spotted with scarlet.

MONARCH.—Cherry red.

VALENTINE MAY.—Pink, striped and dashed with scarlet.

WASHINGTON.—Deep, rich purple, very fragrant.

Monthly Carnations.

PRICE—30 Cents each; $3 per doz.

BEAUTY.—Straw color, striped with pink.

DONADIS PRIDE.—White, tipped with deep rose.

EDWARDSII.—Pure white, large perfect flower.

PURITY.—Very large flower, deep carmine, profuse bloomer.

PRESIDENT DE GRAW.—Pure white, occasionally shaded blush.

VAILLANTE.—Small, bright scarlet, profuse bloomer.

VARIEGATED PURITY.—Carmine, striped.

Pinks.

These have a more dwarfish habit than Carnations, growing only twelve or fifteen inches high, but none the less desirable in the flower-garden. They embrace all the various shades and styles of color found in the Carnation, being very double, and highly clove-scented; plants perfectly hardy. The following embrace a fine collection.

PRICE—30 Cents each; $3 per doz.

ANNOTDALE,
BRUNETTE.
EARL CARLISLE.
ERNEST.
ESTHER.
FANCY.
GENERAL LA FAYETTE.
NINA.
PUMILLA.
QUEEN OF PINKS.
SARAH HOWARD.—Pure white, one of the most desirable.

Hardy Herbaceous Flowering Plants.

We have made a large addition to our collection of this class of plants. They are hardy and easily cultivated, and will thrive in any common soil, flowering from May to October.

PRICE—30 Cents each.

ACHILLEA TOMENTOSA.—Golden yellow.

ACONITUM, (Monkshood.)—Variegated.

ASTILIBE JAPONICA.—Pure white feather-like flowers, in dense spike form.

BELLIS, OR DAISIES.—(See Bedding out Plants.)

CARNATIONS.—(See Special List.)

CHRYSANTHEMUMS.—(See Special List.)

CLEMATIS, AMERICAN, (Climbing plants.)—White flowering, blooms in August.

CLEMATIS, VITICELLA.—Blue flowered.

CLEMATIS, FLORIDA.—Has large rose like, double white flowers, sweet scented.

CLEMATIS, SWEET SCENTED.—Has white flowers, very fragrant.

DELPHINUM BELLA DONNA.

DELPHINUM, FORMOSUM.—Deep sky blue, white center.

DELPHINUM, HERMAN STENGER.

DIANTHUS BARBATUS, (SWEET WILLIAM.)—A fine assortment.

DIELYTRA SPECTABLIS.—Has racemes, heart shaped, red flowers.

GALIUM SYLVATICUM.—Beautiful feathery white flower.

HEMEROCALLIS, (or Day Lilies,) FLAVA.

HEMEROCALLIS, SIEBOLDII.

HEMEROCALLIS, SIEBOLDII VARIEGATA.

LILIES.—(See Bulbous Roots.)

LOBELIA, PALUDOSA.

LOBELIA, SYPHILITICA.

LYCHNIS, FULGENS.

NEUROLAMIA ARIBIDIFLORA.

PÆONIA.—(See Special List.)

PANSIES.—(See Bedding-out plants.

PAPAVER, BRACTEATUM.—Scarlet, very large and showy.

PAPAVER, COCCINEUM.—Beautiful orange; blooms all the summer.

PAPAVER, ORIENTAL.—Red, very large flower.

PHLOX.—(See Special List.)

PRIMULA.—(Polyanthus,) Of several colors.

PYRETHRUM.—(Double Feverfew,) (See Bedding-out Plants.)

POLEMONIUM REPTANS.

SPIREA FILIPENDULA PLENA.

SPIREA ULMARIA VARIEGATA.

SILENE MINIATA.

VERONICA AUSTRIACA.

VERONICA GENTIONOIDES.—Pale blue.

VIOLA.—(Sweet scented Violet.) (See Bedding-out Plants.)

VINCA.—Variegated leaved, sky blue flowers.

Bulbous Flower Roots.

Imported annually from Holland.

The following choice collection of Bulbs has been selected with especial reference to their fine blooming habits, brilliant colors, and exquisite fragrance. Their quality cannot be surpassed. They are greatly superior to those refuse roots sent out annually for public sale in our large cities. All who wish to obtain one of the best assortments will find it very much to their advantage to avail themselves of the opportunity which, by importation, we annually offer them.

These Bulbs answer for forcing in the winter, for the parlor, as well as for planting out in the garden. They are always warranted to be sound, and true to name and color, and will be sold as low as they can be obtained elsewhere.

Directions.—The preferable season for planting out Bulbs is from October until the freezing up of the ground. The depth that they should be buried varies with varieties. Hyacinths, Large Lilies, Crown Imperials, and Narcissus, four inches; Tulips, double Narcissus, and Jonquils, three inches; Crocus, and Snow-drops, four inches; always measuring from the top of the Bulb. Every other year, Hyacinths, Tulips, &c., should be taken up and separated. The time is about one month after the bloom is completely gone, when the plants assume a yellowish appearance. Cut off the stem within one inch of the Bulb, but leave the fibres on, then spread them in an airy room to dry for several weeks; after which they should be laid away in dry sand, or wrapped closely in paper, until the planting season returns.

AMARYLLIS.—The Amaryllis are large strong bulbs. They succeed well when planted in May. They are tender, and should be taken up in the fall, dried, and laid away where they may be exempt from frost.

AMARYLLIS, ALTISSIMA.—Most splendid red, very beautiful. $2.

AMARYLLIS, BELLADONNA MAJOR.—Large, pale violet and white, very showy. $2.

AMARYLLIS, FORMOSISSIMA.—Rich velvety crimson. 50c.

CROCUS.—Crocus should be planted in September or October. It is a hardy plant, gorgeously enameling the garden or lawn in early spring with its abundant flowers of varied hue. Price—25c. per doz., $1.50 per 100.

CROCUS, BLUE.—Very fine.

CROCUS, CLOTH OF GOLD.—Bright yellow.

CROCUS, DAVID RIZZIO.—Purple, fine.

CROCUS, LARGE YELLOW.—Very large and fine.

CROCUS, PURPLE.

CROCUS, QUEEN VICTORIA.—Very large, white.

CROCUS, VIOLET STRIPED.

CROCUS, WHITE.—Very fine.

CROWN IMPERIAL.—This bulb throws up a strong stem three or four feet high, producing a crown of beautiful bell-shaped flowers in April or May. It is hardy. The assortment embraces several varieties. Price—38 to 50 cents each; $3 to $4 per dozen.

GLADIOLUS.

The Gladiolus is the most beautiful of our Summer Bulbs, with tall spikes of flowers, some two feet or more in height, and often several from the same bulb. The flowers are of almost every desirable color.

The following list comprises but a portion of our stock.

PRICE—25 to 50 cts.; or $2.50 to $4 per doz., except where noted.

ADONIS.—Light cherry color, lower division yellowish, with bright carmine stains.

APOLLON.—Large flower of a perfect shape, rosy lilac, with a large stain of light rose, finely striped with white in the center. 50c. each.

BELLE GABRIELLE.—Large flower, perfect shape, very fresh lilac colored rose, slight blazed with bright rose,

BRENCHLEYENSIS.—Bright deep scarlet.

CERES.—Pure white, stained with purplish rose; large flower, very fine stalk.

CHARLES DICKENS.—Very delicate rose, tinted with chamoise, blazed and striped with carminate bright rose. 75c. each.

CHERUBINI.—Large flower, perfect shape, white ground, largely blazed with carminate violet. 75c. each.

COMTE DE MORNY.—Dark cherry red, large white stains, striped with purple.

COURANTI FULGENS.—Bright brilliant crimson; fine shaped flower.

DR. ANDRY.—Very bright orange.

DR. LINDLY.—Very large and well opened flower, perfect shape, ground tender rose, blazed with carminate cherry color. $1 each.

EDULIA.—Middle-sized and very well opened flower; lower division white, stained with violet, the upper divisions striped with white lines; beautiful. 75c. each.

ELDORADO.—Fine pure yellow, the interior divisions striped with red.

EURYDICE.—Large flower, perfect shape, pure white, blazed with carminate rose. $1.50 each.

FELICIEN DAVID.—Large flower, perfect shape, cherry-rose, striped with light carmine on large white ground. $1 each.

JAMES WATT.—Very large and well opened flower; light vermilion, stains very pure white, striped with delicate rose. 75c. each.

JOANNE D'ARC.—White, very slightly tinted with rose, striped and stained with carminate purple.

JOHN BULL.—Ivory white; large and fine.

LA QUINTINIE.—Light orange; of a fine effect.

LEONARD DE VINCI.—Purplish rose, stains delicately striped with carminate rose on aurora colored ground; new color. 75c. each.

LORD BYRON.—Very bright scarlet, stained and ribboned with pure white; very showy plant. $1 each.

LORD GRANVILLE.—Straw color, stained with deep yellow, and striped with red.

MAC MAHON.—Orange colored, cherry rose, satin-like or glazed, red striped.

MADAME BASSEVILLE.—Large, cherry-colored flower, purplish stains, on a white yellowish ground, with lines in the middle of each division.

MADAME DE VATRY.—White, slightly sulphurish, stains purplish carmine; very large flower.

NAPOLEON III.—Very bright scarlet, red striped in the center of the divisions; very fine flower.

NEPTUNE.—Very beautiful red, variegated and stained with carmine.

NEWTON.—Large flower, perfect shape, dark crimson red, with white ground; new shade, very fine. $1 each.

PENELOPE.—Large flower, slightly carnation colored, interior divisions tinted with yellow, carmine striped.

PETER LAWSON.—Rosy or purplish lilac, very large white stains; shade new and charming.

PLUTO.—Deep scarlet, white stains shaded violet purple.

PRINCE IMPERIAL.—Very vigorous plant, very large flower, white, lightly flesh colored, stains very large, carminate violet.

REBECCA.—White, slightly variegated with lilac. 40c. each.

REINE VICTORIA.—Very large and well opened flower, pure white, stained carminate violet; very hardy and vigorous. 75c. each.

REVEREND BERKLEY.—Large flower, of good shape, disposed in large spikes, light rose, tinted with violet and carminate striped on white ground. $1 each.

ROI LEOPOLD.—Rose, very slightly orange colored and blazed, very firm white stains. $1 each.

RUBENS.—Light vermilion color, very bright, stains striped with carmine on whitish ground.

SHAKESPEARE.—Very large flower, perfect shape, white, very slightly blazed with carminate rose, very large, rosy stains. $2 each.

SIR JOSEPH PAXTON.—Large flower, perfect shape, white, very slightly tinted with light orange color, finely striped with carminate red on white ground; very brilliant color. $1.50 each.

SIR WM. HOOKER.—Very large and well opened, perfect shape, light cherry color, rose carmine stains on pure white ground. $1.50 each.

TRIOMPHE D' ENGHIEN.—Carminate, lightly stained and washed with yellow.

VESTA.—Pure white, stained with purplish carmine on yellow ground.

HYACINTHS.—Double and single, of the greatest variety of colors. They begin to flower in April and continue nearly a month in bloom. We import annually. Named sorts, double and single, $2 to $3 per dozen; mixed, $2 per dozen.

JONQUILS, DOUBLE.—Per dozen, $1.

JONQUILS, SWEET SCENTED.—Per dozen, 75 cts.

LILIES.—Few plants are more attractive than the Lily. It produces a gorgeous display either in doors or out; and as it is quite hardy, may be liberally planted in the open border, and thus constitute one of our finest autumnal plants. A good collection of the finest sorts.

LILIUM, AURATUM.—Pure white, with gold yellow stripes and lilac-crimson spots. $1.00 each.

LILIUM, CANDIDUM.—White, fragrant blossoms. 25c. each.

LILIUM, EXCELSUM.—Buff yellow, very fragrant. 50c. each.

LILIUM, EXIMIUM.—Pure white, 3 to 4 feet, very effective; free-blooming, long flower. 75c. each.

LILIUM, SPECIOSUM LANCIFOLIUM ALBUM.—Pure white. 50c. each.

LILIUM, SPECIOSUM LANCIFOLIUM RUBRUM.—White, with crimson spots. 30c. each.

LILIUM, SPECIOSUM LANCIFOLIUM ROSEUM.—White, with rose spots. 30c. each.

NARCISSUS, (Daffodil.)—The Narcissus is a very fine spring flowering bulb, and indispensable to a fine collection. As they are hardy they need not be taken up oftener than to part the roots; once perhaps in two or three years. Price—Best named sorts, 25 cents each, $2 per dozen.

SNOWDROPS, (Galanthus Nivalis.)—This is the earliest of all the garden tribe, often lifting its head above the new fallen snow as if in defiance of its rival purity and whiteness. Every third year the roots should be taken up in June or July, and kept in a dry place till August, when they may be re planted. Best double sorts, 75 cts. per doz.

TIGER FLOWERS, (Ferraria.)—Flowers very beautiful, continuing to bloom a long time. Plant in May, two inches deep; take up in October, dry the bulbs and keep from frost. Price—20 Cents each; $2 per dozen.

TUBE ROSES.—Bloom on tall stems in the autumn, the flowers creamy white, and very fragrant. Price—15 Cents each; $1.25 per dozen.

TULIPS.—The Tulip is a flower of easy cultivation. The season for planting is in October.

TULIPS, BYBLOEMS.—Per doz., $1.

TULIPS, BIZARRES.—Per doz., $1.

TULIPS, DOUBLE EARLY.—Named varieties, per doz., $1.50.

TULIPS, DOUBLE MIXED.—Without names, per doz., $1.

TULIPS, DOUBLE LATE.—Named varieties, per doz., $1.50.

TULIPS, PARROT.—Good mixed varieties, per doz., $1.

TULIPS, SINGLE EARLY,—Named varieties.—Per doz., $1.

TULIPS, SINGLE VARIETIES.—Mixed without names. 75 cts.

Dahlias.

The following list of Dahlias presents a choice selection. They have all been flowered upon our own grounds, and can be relied upon as being *true to name.*

Dahlias require a rich, mellow, well under-drained soil; they should be liberally treated with well rotted stable manure. To keep the ground sufficiently moist, let it be thoroughly mulched; this is better than the continued application of water. In a very dry time, water applied once a week may be well. Superfluous branches should be thinned out, and the stems secured to strong stakes. In the winter, the roots should be kept dry, and free from frost. They may be planted as late as the middle of June; and the roots secured for the winter in October or November.

PRICE—Whole, well grown roots, 25 Cents each; $2 per dozen.

ADELINE.—Chrome yellow, striped with rose.

ADMIRAL DUNDAS, (Lawton.)—Salmon buff, fine form.

AGINCOURT, (Fellows.)—Rosy purple, fine petal.

AMAZONE.—Superb yellow, margined with scarlet.

AMPHION.—Orange, laced with crimson.

ANNE SALTER, (Salter.)—Delicate waxy pale peach.

ANNIE, (Rawlings.)—Fine lilac form, excellent.

ANTAGONIST.—Pure white.

ANTICIPATION.—Pale lilac.

ANTOINETTE.—Blush, edges lightly touched with purple.

ARCHBISHOP OF CANTERBURY.—Crimson maroon, shaded with purple.

ARIEL.—Pure white.

ATTRACTION.—White and crimson.

BARON ANDERSON, (Perry.)—Bright orange, tipped with white, constant.

BARMAID.—White, beautifully edged with pink.

BARONNE DE MELO.—Lilac pink, large, and profuse bloomer.

BARTONIA.—Crimson.

BEAUTY OF THE BATH, (Blush.)—Deep rich yellow, medium size, fine.

BEAUTY OF THE GROVE.—Salmon buff, tipped with purple.

BEAUTY OF SUSSEX.—Rose, edged with crimson.

BELLE DE NOGENT.—White, splashed with crimson.

BELLE DE PARIS.—Blush, tipped with lavender; large and fine.

BISHOP OF HEREFORD.—Crimson maroon, fine.

BLACK DIAMOND.—Very deep crimson velvety maroon, almost as dark as Essex Triumph; a superb flower, peculiar foliage.

BRILLIANT.—Scarlet.

CHAMELEON.—Orange yellow, striped with scarlet, and tipped with white.

CAPRICE, (Felive.)—Pale yellow, lightly edged with rosy amaranth, fine.

CAPT. INGRAHAM, (Stein).—Very dark crimson, large, fine form; splendid.

CELINE.—Yellow, superb flower.

CHERUB.—Bright orange, novel shade, fine form.

CHRISTOPHE SCHMIDT, (Deegan).—Orange, fine form, large.

CLEOPATRA.—Orange yellow, striped with crimson, scarlet.

COCKATOO, (Walters).—Deep pure purple, with white tip, fine showy flower.

COMET, (Keynes).—Yellow ground, with pink edge; extra.

CORSAIR, (Turner).—Deep red, fine form.

CRITERION, (Miller).—Orange scarlet, very large and attractive.

CUCKOO, (Salter).—Purple, tipped with white, fancy flower, finely variegated; extra.

DHWALA GIRL.—Self color, crimson scarlet; splendid.

DIADEM.—Dark maroon.

DIDON, (Miquet).—Yellow, tipped with white.

DOUGLAS JERROLD.—Orange yellow, edged with bronze red.

DUCHESS BRABANT.—Purple, pointed with white.

DUCHESS OF KENT.—Yellow, tipped with white, fine.

DUCHESS OF WELLINGTON, (Turner).—Soft pale cream color; very fine.

DUKE OF CAMBRIDGE.—Silvery lilac.

DUKE OF ROHAN.—Bright vermillion.

EDWARD MILLER.—Yellow, bordered with red.

ELDORADO.—Pale, golden yellow.

EMPRESS, (Proctor).—White, shaded with peach lilac, constant.

ESSEX TRIUMPH.—Deep sombre maroon, the very darkest; fine form

EUGENIE, (Addis).—Finest purple, tipped with white, constant.

FANNY KEYNES.—Buff, tipped with crimson.

FLORAL BEAUTY.—Crimson, shaded with pink; beautiful.

FLORENCE NIGHTINGALE, (Dodd).—Buff, tipped with white; superb.

FORGET-ME-NOT.—Crimson, tipped with white.

FREDERICK HOFFMAN.—Deep rose, edged with white.

FREDERICK JEROME.—Rich violet purple.

GARLINGO.—Purple, shaded with crimson; unsurpassed.

GASPARINE.—Maroon and white.

GEM OF THE GROVE.—Dark maroon.

GEN. BOSQUET, (Belet).—Saffron yellow, pointed with rosy amaranth.

GEN. FANCHER.—Cinnamon, shaded with crimson.

GOLDSMITH, (Keynes).—Clear yellow, fine form.

GRAND DUKE.—Bluish lilac, rare color, very superior.

GRANTAS GEM.—Fine orange.

GRANT THORBURN.—Rosy lilac; superb.

GRAND SULTAN, (Turner).—Very dark crimson maroon; extra fine.

HAIDEE, (Miquel).—Bronzed lilac, with gold points, good form; novel.

HON. MRS. HERBERT.—Amber, shaded with crimson.

INDISPENSABLE YELLOW.—Good form.

JAUNE DE PASSEY.—Very full, beautiful yellow.

JENNY LIND.—Ruby purple, ti ped with peach blush.

KING OF WHITES, (Smith).—A superior clear white.

KING OF YELLOWS.—Pale yellow; superb.

LADY CATHCART.—Blush white, tipped with purple; one of the best.

LADY FLORA.—Yellow, tipped with crimson.

LADY FOLKSTONE, (Keynes).—Buff yellow, tipped with purple; first rate.

LADY MARY LAROUCHERE.—White, tipped with lavender.

LA ROSIER.—Rosy lilac, spotted with crimson.

LEADER.—Purple lilac, striped with crimson.

LILAC KING.—Fine lilac.

LORD BATH, (Wheeler.)—Deep crimson maroon, superb flower

LORD BYRON.—Salmon.

LORD PALMERSTON, (Holmes).—Deep crimson scarlet, fine flower.

LUDWIG PEMSEL.—Maroon, beautifully edged with white.

MADAMOISELLE BRIMEUX.—Blush white, bordered with white.

MAD. ALFRED PERIGNON, (Basseville).—Rosy salmon, shaded with white.

MAD. ROSSIN.—Light saffron, striped with red.

MAD. ZAHLER.—Buff, tipped with red.

MALAKOFF.—Vivid scarlet, large flower.

MARECHAL PELISSIER, (Miquet).—Golden yellow, bordered with carmine.

MARY.—Pure white; a beauty.

MIDNIGHT.—Black, shaded with purple, fine.

MISS BATHURST.—Lilac, tipped with white; a novelty.

MISS CAROLINE.—White, slightly tipped with purple; splendid.

MISS CHAPLIN.—Peach pink, tipped with crimson purple.

MISS FRAMPTON, (Rawlings).—Blood red, tipped with white; unrivaled fancy flower.

MISS VYSA.—White, tipped with lilac.

MISS BURDETT COUTTS, (Turner).—Fawn, short stout petals, exquisite form.

MISS WENTWORTH.—Blush white, tipped with rosy pink; extra.

MONS. CHAIX.—Deep orange.

MONT BLANC.—Pure white, best of the whites, large.

MRS. CHARLOTTE MASON.—Beautiful blush white, remarkably close and well formed.

MRS. HANSARD.—Yellow, tipped with white.

MRS. JAMES.—Buff red, tipped with white.

MRS. RAWLINGS.—Blush, beautiful wax-like petals, fine.

MRS. SELDON.—Sulphur yellow.

MRS. SPARY, (Keynes).—Salmon, blush tip, novel.

MRS. STOWE, (Dodd).—Blush, very fine, extra.

MRS. WHEELER, (Wheeler).—Rich deep scarlet, solid fine flower.

NAPOLEON III, (Sieckmann).—Orange scarlet.

NEPALENSE CHIEF.—Yellow and crimson.

OMER PACHA.—Bright red.

PHÆTON.—Rose, striped with crimson.

PIGEON, (Dr. Kniff.)—Rosy bronze, tipped with white; one of the finest.

PRE-EMINENT, (Fellows).—Rich, deep purple, extra fine form.

PRIMROSE INVINCIBLE.—Yellow.

PRINCE JEROME.—Violet purple.

PRINCE NAPOLEON.—Cinnamon, tipped with purple.

PRINCESS CHARLOTTE.—Violet purple, tipped with pure white; extra.

PRINCESS LOUISA.—Shaded salmon.

PRINCESS RADZVILLE.—White, tipped with purple.

QUEEN, (Widnall's.)—Peach lilac.

QUEEN OF BEAUTIES.—White, tipped with lake.

QUEEN OF THE EAST.—Peach blush.

QUEEN OF WHITES.—Pure white, fine form.

QUEEN VICTORIA.—Yellow, distinctly margined with red, fine showy flower; very large.

REINE VICTORIA, (Roinet.)—White, bordered with lilac; splendid showy flower.

RING-LEADER, (Holmes.)—Bright ruby, petal and outline perfect.

ROBERT BRUCE, (Bush.)—Orange scarlet, exquisite form, large.

ROI LEOPOLD, (Cailloux.)—Brilliant orange scarlet, large and splendid.

ROI DE PONTILLE.—Crimson, maroon edge, fine.

ROSEA ELEGANS.—Rosy lilac, exquisite form, splendid.

RUBY QUEEN, (Keynes.)—Bright clear ruby, splendid form and constant.

RUGEREENS GRATIILIST.—Dark crimson.

SATIRIST.—Crimson, shaded with purple.

SEBASTOPOL.—Brilliant scarlet, very large.

SHYLOCK.—Fine, scarlet, good form.

SIR CHARLES NAPIER.—Unsurpassed red.

SIR F. BATHURST.—Crimson fine.

SIR ROBERT PEEL.—Scarlet, noble flower.

SIR R. WHITTINGTON.—Ruby crimson.

SPOT, (Keynes.)—Lilac, spotted with white, fine.

STANDARD BEARER.—Dark puce, a new color, deep, closely flowered good outline.

STERN VON MEIDLING.—Yellow.

STRIATA FULGENS.—Sulphur yellow, spotted and striped with pink

SUMMIT OF PERFECTION.—Dark velvety purple, superb.

SURPRISER, (Oakley.)—Dark crimson, tipped with white, constant

TRIOMPHE DE LANNOY.—Bluish lilac, pointed with white.

TRIOMPHE MAGDEBURG.—Scarlet, tipped and striped with white.

TRIOMPHE RAMBOIX.—Amber, shaded with rose, tipped with white

UNANIMITY.—Scarlet and deep yellow, flaked or striped.

WAR EAGLE.—Deep rich scarlet, showy flower.

WHITE STANDARD.—Small white flower, shaded lilac.

YELLOW BEAUTY, (Turner.)—Bright yellow, good form and constant.

YELLOW SUPERB.—Fine yellow, exquisite form.

Additional List.--Dahlias.

ALLIANCE.
BARONNE LAMARTINE.
BEESWING.
CLAUDE LORAINE.
DUTCH GOLDFINCH.
GEORGE VILLARS.
GRENADIER.
HARBINGER.
MARIA CARTER.
MASTERPIECE.
MADAME ELIZA SMELLY.
OPHIRE.
PLAISANCE.
REINE DES ROSES.
SIR JOHN FRANKLIN.
STAR.
YELLOW STANDARD.

Lilliputian, or Bouquet Dahlias.

PRICE—30 cts. each ; $3 per dozen.

This novel section includes a valuable class of varieties, distinguished by a profusion of elegant miniature blossoms, remarkable for their symmetry of form, and beauty of color. They deserve a permanent place in every collection.

ALBA FLORIBUNDA NANA.—White, profuse bloomer.

ANNIE.—Blush, crimson edge.

BESSIE.—Buff, shaded red.

BLACK DIAMOND.—Maroon.

BLACK DWARF.—Dark maroon.

CONQUEROR.—Orange and scarlet.

DEUTSCHE NEUHEIT.—Crimson, with orange tips.

DEUTSCHER GOLDFINK.—Yellow, orange tipped.

DR. SCHWEBBS.—Dark crimson.

DR. STEIN.

ESTHER.—Yellow, tipped with white.

FREDERICK KIND.—White, tipped rosy purple.

GERMAN BOY.—Cinnamon.

GRAFULA.—Blush, striped and spotted carmine.

GROS VON TRECKEN.—Crimson and scarlet.

HERTHA VON BONIN.—Purplish violet, white ground.

HERTZOGIN VON ORLEANS.—Pale yellow and crimson.

JOHANNA WAGNER.

KLEINE BRANT.—White, tipped with purplish carmine.

KLEINER HERMANN.—Pale cherry, pointed with white.

KLEINER ROSENBRAUT.—Pale lilac, with yellow center.

LILLIPUT KŒNIGIN.

LILLIPUT MOHR.—Dark maroon.

LITTLE BEAUTY.—Blush, crimson edged.

LITTLE CHARLES.—Amaranth and orange.

LITTLE DEAR.—Blush, marbled with purple.

LITTLE KATE.—Deep purple, fine form; extra.

LITTLE FRED.—Blush, mottled crimson.

LITTLE NYMPH.—Pure white, shaded rose.

LITTLE WILLIE.—Rich deep pink.

LITTLE WONDER.—Crimson scarlet.

MEINE STREFLING.—Salmon, striped crimson.

MOONBEAM.—White, lilac center.

PEARL.—Pure white.

PENELOPE.—Blush, purple tipped.

PERFECTION.—Deep maroon, fine form.

PRINCESS OF LILLIPUTS.—Blush, amber shaded.

PURPLE GEM.—Rich purple.

PET OF THE VILLAGE.

SCHMIDT'S GEM.—Violet and crimson.

SELMER.—Yellow, purple tip.

Select Verbenas.

The Verbena is decidedly one of the richest acquisitions to the flower garden; it blooms in great profusion during the Summer and Autumn, continuing until the ground becomes hard frozen. It looks bright and vigorous always, not being affected by the sudden changes of temperature or moisture. As it is a trailing plant, covering the ground closely, it is finely adapted for grouping, or for mounds. The following include the best and most rare varieties.

Select Collection of Verbenas.

PRICE—15 Cents each; $1.25 per dozen; $8 per hundred.

ACHILLES.—Blue, very dark center.

ACME.—Deep maroon, yellow eye.

ADA.—Blush ground, deep carmine eye.

AMETHYST.—Deep carmine, white eye.

AMELIA.—Variegated, crimson and white.

ALEMA.—Deep salmon.

ARIEL.—Dark blue, white eye.

BANDERO.—Violet, maroon and white.

BIANEA.—White, carmine eye.

BIJOU.—Deep indigo blue, fragrant.

BIZARRE.—Scarlet and white; extra.

BLACKAMOOR.—Crimson maroon.

BLACK DIAMOND.—Darkest maroon; extra.

BLUE BIRD.—Large, deep blue.

BORDALBAN.—Purplish blue, white center.

BOULE DE NEIGE.—White, very fine.

BOUQUET.—Pink, crimson center; very large.

BRIGHTNESS.—Scarlet crimson.

BRILLIANT DE VAISE.—Scarlet, profuse bloomer.

CAROLINE.—Blush, mottled and speckled crimson.

CHARLIE.—Purple, white eye, fine and large.

CHERRY RIPE.—Rich cherry color.

CLARA.—Carmine, pink and white.

CLARET QUEEN.—Violet crimson.

COLLOSSUS.—Crimson, violet eye, size immense

CRAIGMILLER.—Purplish crimson, yellow eye.

DUNBAR.—Deep plum color, white eye.

ECHOLINE.—Light vermilion, yellow eye.

EMELINE.—Pink salmon.

EVA.—Large vermilion, white eye.

EXCELSIOR.—Pure white, tinted rose.

FIRE FLY.—Scarlet, with yellow eye.

FLIRT.—White, blotched and specked crimson.

FOX HUNTER.—Scarlet.

FRAGRANS.—White.

GARNET.—Ruby, white eye.

GETTYSBURG.—Crimson, fine form.

GIGANTIC.—Crimson, very large.

GLEAM.—Rich deep scarlet, white eye.

GLOW-WORM.—Dark pink, yellow eye.

HARKAWAY.—Large, magenta, white eye.

HELEN.—Maroon, white eye.

IMPERATRICE ELIZABETH.—Purple and white stripe

JANE.—Large blue, white eye.

KING OF BLACKS.—Deep maroon.

LADY MELVILLE.—Deep red, white eye.

LAPORTE.—Pink, white eye.

LUCY GRAY.—Pink.

MAGNUM BONUM.—Dark velvety red.

MARY.—Large, crimson, white eye.

MATTIE.—Pure white, rose margin.

MELINDRIS ALBA.—White, fine bedder.

MINOLA.—Rich crimson, yellow eye.

MISS KNIGHT.—Light scarlet, white eye.

MONSTROSA SUPERBA.—Dark violet, yellow eye.

MRS. BLISS.—Rich cherry, yellow center.

MRS. KEYES.—Scarlet, pink and white.

MRS. WILSON.—Crimson, yellow eye.

MRS. WOODRUFF.—Dark scarlet.

PET.—Solferino, white eye.

PLATO.—Maroon, scarlet and white.

PLUTO.—Purple, white eye.

QUEEN OF WHITES.—Pure white, the best.

RICHARD COBDEN.—Violet blue, fragrant.

ROVER.—Blood red, white eye.

SCARLET CHIEF.—The most vivid scarlet.

SCARLET CUSHION.—Scarlet crimson, white eye.

SCARLET DEFIANCE.—Fiery scarlet; one of the best.

SILVER STAR.—Maroon, white eye.

SPLENDOR.—Vermilion, crimson and white.

SUPERBA MAJOR.—Clear white, crimson blotched.

TRIOMPHE.—Pink, tinted scarlet and white.

URALIA.—Salmon, crimson eye.

VELVET MANTLE.—Crimson scarlet, violet shade.

VENUS.—Pink, white eye.

VIRGINALE.—Large, pure white.

WAREGAN.—Fiery scarlet, dark eye.

WARLOCK.—Light rose, shaded maroon.

ZEBRA.—White and purple, striped.

ZULA.—Deep blue, white eye.

Fuchsias.

We invite particular attention to this beautiful tribe of plants. They will bloom from May to November, either in the pot or out of doors. Water them freely when growing, and syringe twice a day during the summer. By putting in cuttings in August, they can be made to flower all winter.

The following list comprises the best new and old sorts.

PRICE—25 Cents each, except where otherwise marked; $2.00 per doz.

Extra large plants 50 Cents each; $4.50 per doz.

ALPHA.—Tube and sepals red, rosy purple carolla, large and fine.

ASPASIA.—Tube and sepals crimson, purple corolla.

BEATRICE.—Sepals white, tipped green, corolla purplish rose.

BEAUTIES BLOOM.—Purple corolla.

BIANCA.—Rosy white sepals, rich pink corolla.

CAROLINA.—Deep crimson, purple corolla.

CATHERINE PARR.—Sepals blush, corolla scarlet.

CHARMING.—Violet corolla, crimson sepals, immense size.

COMMODORE.—Tube and sepals vermilion, corolla splendid purple.

DAY DREAM.—Sepals scarlet carmine, corolla plum color.

DIADEM DE FLORE.—Tube and sepals white, corolla vermilion; fine.

ELM CITY, (Veitch.)—Sepals enclosing, corolla forming rich crimson globular balls, dwarf compact habit, double; extra fine.

FASCINATION.—Double purple corolla, crimson sepals.

GARIBALDI.—Double, dense blue violet corolla.

GLOBOSA.—Tube crimson, corolla purple, small.

GUIDING STAR.—Crimson corolla, white sepals, profuse bloomer. 50 cts.

MARIA CORNELISSON.—Double white corolla, crimson sepals.

MR. BRAEMT.—Double white corolla, carmine sepals. 50 cts.

NARDYE FERES.—Red sepals, pure white corolla. 50 cts.

NORFOLK GIANT.—Immense double, violet.

PICTURATA.—Double white corolla, sepals scarlet.

PRINCE IMPERIAL.—Purple corolla, crimson sepals, beautifully reflexed, dwarfish habit, a profuse bloomer. 50 cts.

PURITANA.—White corolla, carmine sepals. 50 cts.

QUEEN OF WHITES.—Double white corolla.

SENATOR.—Bright, waxy crimson sepals, rich violet corolla.

SIR COLIN CAMPBELL.—Double purple corolla, crimson sepal.

SIR ROBERT PEEL.—Fine large crimson flower, violet corolla.

SNOWDROP.—Tube white, corolla pink, delicate and pretty.

SOUVENIR DE CHISWICK.—Crimson sepals, deep violet corolla.

SPECIOSA.—Sepals blush white, corolla rosy red, large.

STRIATA PERFECTA.—Double, striped blue and crimson.

SYDONIE.—Tube and sepals white, corolla pink, shaded with purple, small.

THE RAJAH.—A fine variety, cornelian.

VENUS DE MEDICI.—Tube white, sepals peach blossom, corolla violet blue; very striking and elegant.

VICTOR EMANUEL.—Sepals coral red, corolla fine double white.

WHITE PERFECTION.—Sepals white, corolla violet.

Salvias.

These produce a fine show of brilliant flowers during the summer season. They are very fine for bedding out.

PRICE—25 Cents each; $2 per dozen.

SPLENDENS, (Scarlet Sage.)—A superb plant for summer decoration, with dense flower spikes of the most brilliant scarlet.

Heliotropes.

Nothing is sweeter than the Heliotrope, and it forms one of the greatest attractions to the flower garden. They are very fine for bedding out.

PRICE—25 Cents each; $2 per dozen.

ALBICANS.—Light, very sweet scented

CORYMBOSUM.—Dwarf, large heads, and sweet flowers.

INTERMEDIA.—Great bloomer and highly scented, good bedding plant.

LIZZIE COOK.—In our estimation the best out; color dark violet purple, white eye, and more fragrant than any other variety.

LUCIEN TARDIFF.—Takes the place of Gem.

SOUVENIR EROUBLY.—Dark color, good habit.

SURPRISE.—Dark purple, very fine grower.

VOLTARIANUM.—Very dark purple, fine.

Petunias.

The Petunia is a fine bedding plant, producing a perfect mass of flowers all Summer. Ours are grown from the best Hybrid varieties.

PRICE—15 Cents each. Per dozen, $1.

Double Petunias.

PRICE—25 Cents each; $2 per dozen.

ADELINE.—Crimson flower, good bloomer.

WILLIAM WHITE.—Crimson, blotched white.

QUEEN OF WHITES.—Pure white.

Summer Climbers.

The following plants are all fine climbers, adapted to trellis work, of rapid growth and free bloomers.

PRICE—25 Cents each; $2 per dozen.

MADEIRA VINE.—Feathery white flowers, fragrance like the Mignonette, very fine for trellis work.

MAURANDIAS.—Blue, white and rose colored.

TROPOEOLUM.—Double, orange.

TROPOEOLUM.—Dark flower.

Miscellaneous Plants.

PRICE—25 Cents each; $2 per dozen, except otherwise noted.

AGERATUM CONSPICUUM ALBUM.—White, flowers in March and April.

AGERATUM MEXICANUM.—Blooms all summer, light blue.

AGERATUM VARIEGATUM.—Light blue.

ALOYSIA CITRIODORA.—Has lemon scented leaves.

ASTERS.—A large assortment seedlings from the best imported seed 50c. per doz.

BALM VARIEGATED.—A hardy perenial, with variegated leaves, novel in appearance, and a delightful fragrance It does particularly well in shaded places.

BOUVARDIA LIANTHA.—Bright scarlet flowers. 50c.

CALCEOLARIAS, (Shrubbery.)—A good collection. 50c.

CINERARIA MARITIMA.—A white foliaged plant, somewhat similar to the centauria, but with leaves deeply cut, and of more vigorous growth.

CUPHEA PLATYCENTRA.—The tube of the flower is scarlet, with the end part white and crimson, having somewhat the appearance of a miniature lighted cigar.

DAISIES.—Double, red and white. Also the Belgic varieties. 15c. each; $1 per dozen.

LANTANA ALBA PERFECTA.—Pure white.

LANTANA CARNEA.—Red and yellow flowers.

LANTANA MAGNA.—Large white, yellow center.

LANTANA MUTABILIS MAJOR.—Orange and scarlet.

LANTANA PICTA SUPERBA.—Straw, lemon eye.

LANTANA RAPHAEL.—Purple, orange and rose.

LANTANA VICTORIA.—White, lemon eye.

LANTANA WILSONII.—Rose and white.

PANSIES.—A fine selection of American, German and English sorts. 15c. each; $1 per dozen.

PYRETHRUM.—(Feverfew,) Double white flowering.

SWEET SCENTED VIOLETS, DOUBLE BLUE NEAPOLITAN.

SWEET SCENTED VIOLETS, DOUBLE WHITE NEAPOLITAN.

SWEET SCENTED VIOLETS, QUEEN OF VIOLETS.—Very double, large and exceedingly fragrant; color white, back petals blue.

SWEET SCENTED VIOLETS, THE CZAR.—Rich bluish purple, large and fragrant.

TRITOMIA UVARIA.—A beautiful garden plant, with spike formed flowers of scarlet and orange color; blooms from July to October. 50c.

VERONICA ANDERSONII.—Lilac, very beautiful.

Coleus.

PRICE—25 Cents each; $2 per dozen.

ALBERT VICTOR.—Center purplish red, broad yellow margin.

BARESII.—Chocolate foliage, margined with light green,

BEAUTY.—Rich velvety purple, margined with pale green.

BLUMEII.—Bright red center, margined with bright golden yellow.

GILSONII.—Dark chocolate, deep green ground.

HER MAJESTY.—Bronze red center, greenish yellow margin.

MARMCRATA.—Foliage yellowish green, marbled with red.

PRINCESS ROYAL.—Center reddish bronze, light yellow edge.

SAUNDERSII.—Foliage chocolate purple, mottled with green.

SETTING SUN.—Rich bronze, crimson center, bright golden edge.

VERSCHAFFELDTII.—Rich velvety crimson.

VEITCHII.—Foliage light green, with chocolate spot.

Achyranthus.

PRICE—25 Cents each; $2 per doz.

AUREUS RETICULATUS.—A "sport," from A. Verschaffeldt, which it resembles in every respect, save in the leaf marking, which, instead of the dark crimson of Verschaffeldtii, is light green, marked with a network of yellow.

VERSCHAFFELDTII.—Foliage a deep crimson, the stem a deep shade of pink.

LINDENII.—Leaves deep blood red color, reflecting varying tints of red and purple.

Geraniums or Pelargoniums.

Of this very beautiful class, we find it so difficult to give any description that conveys any distinctive idea of their character, that we have selected the following varieties as possessing the greatest variety of colors, combined with compactness of habit and free-blooming qualities.

PRICE—30 Cents to 50 Cents each; $3 to $5 per doz.

AGNES.
BEAUTY.
BEADSMAN.
BIANCA.
BRIDEGROOM.
BRIDAL RING
CAPTIVATION.
CONSTANTINE.
COSTELLO.
LILACEA.
MAZEPPA.
MAZINELLA
MISS PERCIVAL.
NORMA.
PERI.
PRINCE ROYAL.
SIR JOSEPH PAXTON.
TAMORLANE.

COUNTESS OF DEVON.

ECLIPSE.

GEN. TAYLOR.

HUMEII.

LADY MARY FOX.

LAVINA.

UNIQUE MILLIZE.

UNION VILLAGE.

VIRGINIA.

WAVERLY.

ZELINDA.

Scarlet and Crimson Geraniums.

PRICE—25 Cents each, or $2.50 per doz.

BALL OF FIRE.—Bright scarlet, immense truss, globular in form, the best.

COMMANDER-IN-CHIEF.—Light scarlet, beautifully marked foliage.

DR. LINDLEY.—Orange scarlet, white eye and very perfect flower; beautiful.

GENERAL GRANT.—Dazzling scarlet, large truss, free bloomer.

HORTENSIS.—Light scarlet, fine bloomer, strong grower.

LIVIATA.—Orange scarlet, profuse bloomer; one of the best.

REBECCA.—Cherry red, dwarf habit, free bloomer, beautiful.

STELLA.—Bright crimson, large truss, dwarfish, free bloomer; extra fine.

VICTOR EMANUEL.—Fine bright scarlet, large white eye.

Salmon, Rose, and White Geraniums.

PRICE—25 Cents each; $2.50 per doz.

BEAUTY.—Salmon changing to white, finely marked foliage.

BICOLOR.—Ground color of flowers nearly white, center making a beautiful salmon.

CHRISTINE.—Deep pink, free bloomer, dwarf habit.

HENRY DE BORDEAUX.—Dark shaded salmon, good bloomer.

LADY MARTIN.—Fine free rosy pink, dwarf habit; excellent for bedding and pot culture.

LUCIA ROSEA.—Light pink; free bloomer, strong habit.

MADAME VOUCHER.—Blush or French white, fine truss.

MIGNON.—Light pink, fine truss, and strong grower.

PHŒNICIAN.—White, center lightly shaded with salmon, beautiful foliage.

PRINCESS ALICE.—Rosy pink, strong habit.

SNOW BALL.—White flowers, dark horse-shoe foliage, robust habit.

Variegated-Leaved Geraniums.

PRICE—30 Cents each; $3 per doz., except where noted.

BIJOU.—Beautiful silver-edged, scarlet flower.

BLACK HAWK.—Bronze black, band very large size.

FLOWER OF SPRING.—White variegation, fine form, dwarfish; one of the best.

FLOWER OF THE DAY.—Yellowish white, variegation; good grower.

LADY COTTINGHAM.—Golden foliage, very handsome.

MOUNTAIN OF SNOW.—Pure white margin; fine.

MRS. MILFORD.—Golden leaf, with a very distinct zone in the center.

MRS. POLLOCK.—Foliage with a very handsome yellow edge, and rich crimson zone; splendid.

SUNSET.—Similar to Mrs. Pollock. 50 cts.

Double Geraniums.

PRICE—30 Cents, except where noted.

AUGUSTA TERNIER.—Light scarlet.

ANDREW HENDERSON.—Deep scarlet, very double and fine. 50c.

EMILE LEMOINE.—Red, with scarlet center.

GLOIRE DE NANCY.—Deep carmine, very double. 50c.

MADAME LEMOINE.—Bright rosy pink. 75c.

TRIUMPH.—Rich shade of scarlet.

TRIUMPH LORRAINE.—Bright cherry carmine.

Scented-Leaved Geraniums.

PRICE—25 Cents each; $2.50 per doz., except where noted.

BALM.

DR. LIVINGSTON.

LADY PLYMOTH.—Silver-edged foliage.

NUTMEG.

PENNYROYAL.

PEPPERMINT.

PIE ODORATA.—Very handsome flowers. 50 cts.

ROSE.

SHRUBLAND PET.—Beautiful green foliage, fine crimson flowers; very handsome for pot culture.

Plants and Vines.

FOR VASES AND HANGING BASKETS.

The following embrace a choice selection for the above named purposes:

ABUTILON MESOPOTAMICUM.—A variety of trailing habit, bearing pendulant flowers in great profusion; the deep red calyx contrasts finely with the golden petals. For rock work or vases it is valuable. 25c. each.

ABUTILON THOMPSONII.—One of the finest acquisitions that has been made to our ornamental leaved plants for some time, of an erect graceful habit; the leaves are mottled or marked with bright golden yellow, which retain their variegation during the hottest weather. 30c. each; $3 per doz.

ALTERNANTHERAS TRICOLOR.—A genus of plants growing from six to twelve inches in height, of the class known as ornamental foliaged plants, to which designation their beautiful leaf tints well entitle them. Well adapted for baskets or vases. Leaves tinted green, crimson and straw color. 30c.

ALTERNANTHERAS VERSICOLOR.—Leaves tinted light rose to deep carmine. 20c. each; $2 per doz.

CENTAUREA CANDIDA.—A valuable plant to contrast with Coleus. Leaves downy white, forming a neat, compact bush. Massed, either with Coleus or Achyranthus, or both, it produces a most pleasing effect. 40c. each.

CENTAUREA GYMNOCARPA.—Attains a diameter of two feet, forming a graceful, rounded bush of silvery gray. Nothing is so well fitted to contrast in ribbon lines with dark foliaged plants. As a plant for hanging baskets, it is also unsurpassed, its drooping fern-like leaves being very effective. 40c. each.

CISSUS DISCOLOR.—One of the finest trailing plants. 30c. each; $3 per doz.

FERNS.—A beautiful foliaged class of plants, well adapted for vase and basket or rockwork. 25c. each; 2.50 per doz.

KENILWORTH IVY.—A fine ivy foliaged trailer. 20c. each; $1.50 per doz.

LOBELIAS.—A fine collection, combining several colors. 20c. each; $1.50 per doz.

LOPHOSPHERNUM SCANDENS.—Vigorous summer climber, with long trumpet-shaped rose-colored flowers. 25c. each; $2.50 per doz.

LYCOPODES.—A fine, delicate foliaged plant with trailing habit; several sorts. 25c. each; $2.50 per doz.

LYSIMACHIA NUMMULARIA, (Moneywort).—A very vigorous trailing plant, with fine foliage and beautiful yellow flowers.

MADERIA VINE.—One of the finest plants for rapidly covering baskets, vases or trellis work. Flowers feathery white, with fragrance of Mignonette. 15c. each; $1 per doz.

MOSS.—A beautiful light green Moss, used for bordering, lining wire baskets, covering vases and rockwork; a vigorous grower with trailing habit. 25c. per square foot.

PEPEROMIA MACULOSA.—The leaves are of a wax-like character, are of great substance, with bright green ribs or veins; beautiful. 30c. each.

PILEA.—Peculiar foliage, with very delicate scarlet flowers.

SEDUM SIEBOLDII.—Variegated. 30c. each.

TROPŒLUMS.—Excellent plants for the flower border in summer, blooming in profusion from June till November. Extensively used for rock work and vases. They bloom best in poor, rocky or sandy soil. 20c. each; $1.50 per doz.

TROPŒLUMS.—Double orange. 20c. each; $1.50 per doz.

TROPŒLUMS.—Dark crimson. 20c. each; $1.50 per doz.

VINCA.—A pretty, variegated leaved, blue flowering plant. 30c.

Green House and Hot House Plants.

ABUTILON, BEDFORDIANUM.—Pale yellow, striped brown, large leaves. 50c.

ABUTILON, STRIATUM.—Beautiful striped. 50c.

ABUTILON, VENOSUM.—Orange, veined with crimson. 50c.

ACHIMENES.—The Achimenes are a beautiful tribe of dwarf plants, and well adapted to windows; their culture is simple, requiring only rich mould and plenty of water. Plant early, and shift several times from small to larger pots as the ball of earth becomes filled with roots. A fine assortment. 30 Cents each.

AGAPANTHUS, UMBELLATA.—Blue, umbel-flowered lily. 50c.

AGAPANTHUS, VARIEGATA.—Variegated. 75c.

ALOE, FOLIIS VARIEGATA.—Variegated leaved. 50c.

ALOE, PICTA.—Painted, fine. 50c.

*BEGONIA, FUCHSOIDES.—Fuchsia like, superb. 30c.

BEGONIA, FUCHSOIDES ALBA.—Fuchsia like, white. 30c.

*BEGONIA, GRANDIFLORA. 30c.

BEGONIA, LEOPOLD.—The best of the collection. 50c.

BEGONIA, MACULATA. 30c.

*BEGONIA, MADAME WAGNER. 30c.

BEGONIA, MANICATA. 30c.

*BEGONIA, REX. 30c.

BEGONIA, RHOMBOIDES.—Rhomboid. 30c.

BEGONIA, SANDRII. 30c.

BEGONIA, SANGUINEA. 30c.

*BEGONIA, SILVER QUEEN. 30c.

*BEGONIA, SIR COLIN CAMPBELL. 30c.

*BEGONIA, ZEBRINA.—Zebra-striped, beautiful. 30c.

CACTUS CEREUS, GRANDIFLORUS.—Night blooming. 30c.

---

*Leaves variegated.

CACTUS CEREUS, HEXAGONUS.—Six angled. 30c.

CACTUS CEREUS, SERPENTINUS.—Snake-like. 30c.

CACTUS CEREUS, TRIANGULARIS.—Large, three-sided. 30c.

CALCEOLARIAS.—(See Bedding Plants.)

CAMELLIAS.—The following list contains a choice collection of Camellias. They are correctly described, so that any one can make his selection with confidence. Price, $1.50 to $3 each.

CAMELLIA, ALBA PLENA.—Pure white, full double, form perfect, petal broad, round and deep; has no superior as a white.

CAMELLIA, ALBA FIMBRIATA.—Pure white, form perfect, edge of each petal fringed.

CAMELLIA, FORDII.—Delicate rose, form perfect, petals numerous and finely arranged; most superb flower.

CAMELLIA, IMBRICATA.—Dark crimson, blotched with pure white; colors very distinct; form perfect, petals round, of great depth, and finely imbricated.

CAMELLIA, INCARNATA, (Lady Hume's Blush).—White, suffused with very delicate rose flowers; perfect, often angular, petals large and deep.

CAMELLIA, JENNY LIND.

CAMELLIA, MARYLANDICA, (Feast's).—Said to be the best scarlet Camellia in cultivation.

CAMELLIA, SARAH FROST, (Ritchie and Dick).—Purple crimson, flowers perfect, petals numerous, broad and neatly arranged.

CAPE JESSAMINE, GARDENA FLORIDA. 30c.

CAPE JESSAMINE, GARDENA FORTUNII. 30c.

CALLA ETHIOPICA. 50c. to $1 each.

CALLA ETHIOPICA NANA.—Dwarf Ethiopian Lily. 50c. to $1 each.

CENTRADENIA GRANDIFLORA.—Very peculiar colored leaf and stem. 30c.

CENTRADENIA ROSEA.—Very fine, delicate foliage and small pink flower. 30c.

CESTRUM NOCTURNUM.—Night-scented Jessamine. 30c.

CINERARIA.—Fine flowering plants from February to May. A large collection. 30 cts. each.

CYPRIPEDIUM INSIGNIS.—Lady slipper, very showy. 50c.

DAPHNE ODORATA. 75c.

DIOSMA FRAGRANS. 30c.

EUONYMUS ALBA, VARIEGATED. 50c.

EUONYMUS AUREA, VARIEGATED. 50c.

EUONYMUS JAPONICA, VARIEGATED. 50c.

EUPATORIUM ARBOREUM. 50c.

EUPATORIUM ELEGANS.—Splendid white flowering. 50c.

EUPHORBIA, SPLENDENS.—Bright rose, profuse bloomer. 30c.

FABIANA, IMBRICATA.—White flowering, table shaped. 30c.

FICUS, ELASTICA.—India Rubber tree. 75c.

FERNS.—A fine collection. 25c. each; $2.50 per doz.

GERANIUMS OR PELARGONIUMS.—(See Special List.)

GERANIUMS, SCARLET AND OTHER COLORS.—(See Special List.)

GERANIUMS, SCENTED-LEAVED.—(See Special List.)

GESNERAS.—A class of plants having a beautiful velvety, high-colored foliage.

GESNERA, CINAPERINE. 30c.

GESNERA, HYBRIDA. 30c.

GESNERA, ZEBRINA. 30c.

HOYA, BELLA.—Pale, wax-like. 75c.

HOYA, CARNOSA.—Very beautiful, wax-like. 30c.

JASMINUM REVOLUTUM.—Large yellow. 30c.

LAVENDULA, DENTATA.—Toothed lavender. 30c.

LYCOPODIUM, CŒSIUM.—Beautiful Chinese. 25c.

LYCOPODIUM, CORDATUM. 25c.

LYCOPODIUM, DENTICULATUM.—Toothed. 25c.

LYCOPODIUM, DUMOSUM. 25c.

LYCOPODIUM, FORMOSUM. 25c.

LYCOPODIUM, LIPODOPHYLLUM. 25c.

PRIMULA, SINENSIS.—Fine assortment. 30c.

ROSMARINUS, ROSEMARY OFFICINALIS. 30c.

SEDUM, PATENS. 15c.

STEVIA, GRANDIFLORA.—White flowering. 50c.

TRADESCANTIA, ZEBRINA.—Zebra-striped. 15c.

YUCCA, FILAMENTOSA.—Fibrous. 50c.

YUCCA, GLORIOSA.—Splendid flowering. 75c.

NOTE.

Every person authorized to act as AGENT for the sale of Stock from this establishment, is furnished with a Certificate from us, duly accrediting him as such.

INDEX.

ORNAMENTAL DEPARTMENT.

CPSIA information can be obtained
at www.ICGtesting.com
Printed in the USA
LVHW030149210323
742063LV00002B/828

9 783382 126360